"Don't you like playing games, Zoe?"

Connel's tone was soft, seductive, disturbing.

She refused to let it get to her. "No, I do not! And stop changing the subject."

"I wasn't. Isn't that what we're talking about? What else could I do but carry you up to bed?"

CHARLOTTE LAMB was born in London, England, in time for World War II, and spent most of it moving from relative to relative to escape bombing. Educated at a convent, she married a journalist, and now has five children. The family lives on the Isle of Man. Charlotte Lamb is the author of more than one hundred books for Harlequin Presents®.

Books by Charlotte Lamb

HARLEQUIN PRESENTS®
1913—THE MARRIAGE WAR
1935—LOVESTRUCK
1949—AN EXCELLENT WIFE?

Don't miss any of our special offers. Write to us at the following address for information on our newest releases.

Harlequin Reader Service
U.S.: 3010 Walden Ave., P.O. Box 1325, Buffalo, NY 14269
Canadian: P.O. Box 609, Fort Erie, Ont. L2A 5X3

CHARLOTTE LAMB

Hot Surrender

TORONTO • NEW YORK • LONDON
AMSTERDAM • PARIS • SYDNEY • HAMBURG
STOCKHOLM • ATHENS • TOKYO • MILAN • MADRID
PRAGUE • WARSAW • BUDAPEST • AUCKLAND

If you purchased this book without a cover you should be aware that this book is stolen property. It was reported as "unsold and destroyed" to the publisher, and neither the author nor the publisher has received any payment for this "stripped book."

ISBN 0-373-12046-X

HOT SURRENDER

First North American Publication 1999.

Copyright © 1999 by Charlotte Lamb.

All rights reserved. Except for use in any review, the reproduction or utilization of this work in whole or in part in any form by any electronic, mechanical or other means, now known or hereafter invented, including xerography, photocopying and recording, or in any information storage or retrieval system, is forbidden without the written permission of the publisher, Harlequin Enterprises Limited, 225 Duncan Mill Road, Don Mills, Ontario, Canada M3B 3K9.

All characters in this book have no existence outside the imagination of the author and have no relation whatsoever to anyone bearing the same name or names. They are not even distantly inspired by any individual known or unknown to the author, and all incidents are pure invention.

This edition published by arrangement with Harlequin Books S.A.

® and TM are trademarks of the publisher. Trademarks indicated with ® are registered in the United States Patent and Trademark Office, the Canadian Trade Marks Office and in other countries.

Look us up on-line at: http://www.romance.net

Printed in U.S.A.

CHAPTER ONE

ZOE usually enjoyed driving home after a long day's work. It gave her a chance to unwind, switch on to automatic pilot because she knew the route so well, then she could let her mind roam free. She often came up with exciting new ideas while she was driving. But tonight she was just that bit too tired, her face very pale against her flame-red hair, her green eyes sleepy. She had been up at five, at the location they were using by six, drinking a polystyrene cup of black coffee as she talked over the scene they were going to shoot with Will, the cameraman, who'd groaned as an ominous blood-red dawn swam up out of the veiled horizon, across misty, mysterious fields.

'I knew it! Look at that sky—red sky in the morning, sailor's warning! Yesterday was so humid, I had a gut feeling a storm was on the way.'

Will was usually right about the weather. Like an animal, he could smell rain coming or a storm brewing, so Zoe had decided to keep working for as long as the weather held off in case they couldn't film outdoors next day. They had filmed until gone seven, when heavy rain began pouring down.

'Have supper with me?' Will had asked, his big blue eyes pleading.

Zoe had sighed, wishing he would stop pursuing her. She liked him a lot, but not in the way he wanted.

'We'll all have supper together,' she'd diplomatically announced, and asked Catering to produce a hot meal.

Will had given her a reproachful look as they all tramped into the on-site caravan where Will slept with his precious cameras. A tall, thick-set man with amazingly well-developed muscles and a rugged face, he always said cameras were female and brooked no rivals which was why he had never married. He had occasionally dated one of the girls working on a film, but his relationships never lasted; his girlfriends always got bored with playing second fiddle to his job.

Zoe hoped that if she kept turning down his invitations he would give up on her. She didn't believe Will was serious; he was just hoping to succeed where others had failed. Zoe's reputation as someone who wasn't a pushover made her a scalp some men would love to hang on their belts. It was getting very boring.

Catering had come up with chilli and rice for them all, perfect wet weather food. The crew had fallen upon it like hungry wolves, but Zoe hadn't eaten; she was dieting. Now she was ravenous, of course. Her stomach rumbled at the thought of food. What did she have in the kitchen which could be cooked in a couple of minutes and wasn't too high in calories? Eggs? Soup?

Glancing at her illuminated dashboard, she saw it was nearly eleven o'clock. Which was more vital—food or sleep? She needed both, equally urgently.

Slowing to take the corner off the main road into the narrow lane leading to her home, she waited, yawning, for a couple of lorries to thunder past.

A man loomed up beside her window out of the dark

and rainy night, making her start in shock. Where on earth had he come from?

For a second she thought he was a mirage, conjured up by her weary brain, then he bent down and tried to open her door.

Zoe was a tough, capable woman of thirty-two, used to authority, scared of very little...spiders, maybe, over-shooting her budget, certainly, or running late on a film. Nothing much else—but, perhaps because she was tired, at that instant her nerve-ends prickled until she remembered that she had automatically locked her doors before she started driving.

Discovering this too, the stranger tapped on her window, saying something, mouth opening and shutting, rain running down his face, drowning out his voice.

Zoe leaned over to touch the button which unwound her window electronically just a fraction. 'What do you want?'

His voice was very deep, faintly hoarse, as if he had a cold or smoked too many cigarettes. 'My car has broken down. Could you give me a lift to a garage?'

He was a big man, his thick black hair half hidden by the hood of an old navy anorak, a curly black beard hiding most of his lower face, looking more like a tramp than someone who owned a car. Zoe looked him over, noting that his jeans were ragged and muddy. Even if her instincts hadn't warned her not to trust him she would never have considered giving him a lift. A woman driving alone at night was crazy if she picked up a strange man. Zoe had heard too many horror stories of women who'd done that.

'The nearest garage shuts at nine o'clock,' she crisply

told him. 'There's a telephone box opposite the church, just down the road; you can ring for a taxi from there.'

His black eyes insistently staring into hers, he bit out, 'You can't leave me out here in this rain. I'm already soaked to the skin. I tried the phone box—it's been vandalised. I drove through a village a couple of miles back down this road and saw a pub which looked open. It wouldn't take you long to give me a lift back there.'

'I'll find my mobile phone and ring for a taxi for you,' Zoe said reluctantly.

Groping for her bag on the seat, she unzipped it and felt among the myriad objects she always took with her to work. She pulled out the phone, held it up, showing it to him.

The wind blew rain into his face. Shivering, he said, 'Great. Ask this firm to get here as soon as possible before I die of pneumonia.'

Zoe tapped in her personal code, only to discover that the phone needed charging.

'Sorry, it isn't working,' she said offhandedly, holding it up to show him she wasn't lying. 'I haven't used it since this morning, but the batteries run down even if you don't use it.' She watched rain running down his face like tears, and felt a flash of sympathy. She would hate to be in his position. If he was another woman she wouldn't hesitate to give him a lift, but she wasn't risking it with some strange man.

'Look, I'll ring for a taxi for you the minute I get home,' she promised. 'Just wait here; one will be along before too long.'

He grabbed her door and hung on to it, leaning into

her car in what she felt to be a menacing way. 'How do I know you'll keep your word?'

Zoe's patience ran out. She was tired, her head was aching, she wanted to get home and into bed.

'You'll just have to trust me. Now, get out of my way or I'll drive off with you hanging on to my door—and don't think I won't.'

'Oh, I'm sure you're capable of it!' he muttered, still holding on to her door. 'Have you thought how it will sound in the press, though?'

Zoe was sure he was too clever not to let go once she started driving away, but, just in case, she pressed the electronic button that wound her window up again.

He tried to hold the window down but couldn't stop it closing, and had to snatch his hand away before it got crushed in the mechanism.

She put her foot down on the accelerator and drove off at speed across the main road. In her driving mirror she caught a brief glimpse of him standing in the torrential rain, glaring after her. From this distance he looked about seven foot tall, way over six foot, anyway, with wide shoulders and long, long legs, his wet jeans clamped to them, emphasising the muscled calves and thighs under the clinging cloth. She couldn't deny he was sexy, in a glowering, thuggish sort of way.

She knew women who went wild about men like him. Women who should have more sense. She was not one of them, however.

He reminded her of someone, but she was too tired to work out who as she headed along the narrow country lane leading to her cottage. Within three minutes she saw the red roof of her cottage up ahead, half hidden by the trees shielding her garden.

She had bought Ivydene because of its peaceful setting and the wonderful view of fields and woods which gave you the impression of an uninhabited landscape. In fact there were other houses, hidden among trees and in folds of the countryside, but she had no close neighbours, could see no lighted windows. Tonight she wished she had. The brief encounter with that man had managed to knock her usual self-confidence a little.

Turning into her driveway, she parked right outside the cottage, jumped out, dashed under the shelter of the small, red-tiled porch built around her front door and locked her car from there with her electronic car key. Rain drummed on the porch roof, dripped off the ivy growing up the walls. Zoe stripped off her wax jacket and left it to drip on a hook in the wall. It was far too wet to take indoors. Stepping out of her boots, too, she stood them against the porch wall, then unlocked the front door and went into the cottage, switching on the light in the hall.

For a second she stood, listening, but apart from the sonorous tick of a large Victorian grandfather clock in the hall everything was quiet. She had been living here for three years now. When she'd bought it, the three-bedroomed cottage had been a mess; it had been uninhabited for a year, the roof had leaked, mould had grown on wallpaper, some of the windows had been broken by local boys.

Zoe couldn't afford to pay workmen to renovate it, but whenever she had any free time she worked on it herself, painting, wallpapering, choosing new curtains and carpets. The cottage had been built in the Edwardian era, and the spacious rooms had high ceilings, decorated with plasterwork, elegant little ironwork fireplaces, and solid oak doors. There was a butler's pantry, and a general air of being a miniature country house.

Padding through to the kitchen in her socks, she opened the fridge, quickly inspecting the contents, but nothing much appealed. She wouldn't get to sleep if she ate a large or rich meal at this hour. It would have to be tomato soup and toast. It only took seconds to open a tin, pour the contents into a saucepan and start cooking it. She cut a couple of slices of bread once the soup was on the hob, and slipped them into the toaster.

After that she walked into the sitting room and switched on her answer-machine, smiling as her sister's warm, cheerful voice filled the room.

'Hi, it's me—don't forget the barbecue on Saturday, will you? Around six o'clock. Bring somebody if you like—who's the latest fella? And a bottle of something; lemonade, wine, anything you like.'

In the background the sound of high-pitched screeching rose, combined with a hammering, crashing sound.

'Sing quietly, darling,' Sancha said in the indulgent tone she always used to the little monster she called Flora. Was that ghastly racket meant to be singing? Zoe switched on the realistic electric log fire on the hearth—the central heating kicked in at six o'clock each evening, but it was only background heat and on a night like this she felt she needed more than that, not to mention the illusion of sitting in front of flames.

'Zoe, I've got exciting news for you! I... Don't do that to the cat!' Sancha suddenly said sharply.

Do what, for heaven's sake? The sounds of spitting and yowling competed with Flora's so-called singing.

'Got to go,' Sancha hurriedly said. 'She's trying to pull the cat through the bars of her playpen. Zoe, don't you dare forget and don't be late! See you!' She hung up; there was a whirring sound and another voice began.

'Zoe, please, I've got to see you, surely we can talk this over?'

Zoe fast-forwarded the machine to get rid of the husky voice. It had been fun dating Larry for a few weeks, but that was all it had been for her. Just light-hearted fun. He was a nice enough guy—which was why as soon as he started to turn serious she had told him they must stop seeing each other. It was kinder to end it before his feelings got out of hand. In the past she had sometimes hesitated and let a relationship go on too long. Zoe didn't want to hurt anyone, but neither was she being black-mailed into bed by someone she didn't love.

The trouble was, Larry wouldn't go away. Since she'd told him she didn't want to see him again he had rung her several times a day, and kept writing her the sort of letters that burn the paper they're written on but are embarrassing to read if you don't feel the same way. Zoe was worried by the bitterness creeping in among the passionate prose.

It wasn't as if she was the first woman in his life; he had had other girlfriends. She knew all about them because he had insisted on telling her every detail of his relationships before her. She hadn't wanted to hear any of it.

She had liked Larry at first, he had seemed fun, but her discovery about his obsession with his past affairs was the first moment when she began to go off him. Zoe never talked about one man to another. She hated having the past hanging around; she switched off memories like a television set and walked away. Life was now, today, the future always beckoned—the past was another country, one she had left behind. Why waste time on what had gone and wouldn't come back? she had told Larry, who had laughed, sounding almost triumphant, and asked her if she was jealous. She didn't need to be, he'd said. None of his earlier girlfriends had meant as much to him as she did. She was the one he had been looking for all his life. He would die rather than lose her.

It was at that moment that Zoe had decided to tell him goodbye. It was all getting too intense for her. A pity she hadn't picked up on his nature earlier. She would never have gone out with him in the first place if she'd known he was so obsessive. It was himself he was obsessed with, that she was sure about, but at the moment he was pinning his self-obsession on her, which was distinctly weird. She found weird people scary, and wished she had never met him.

But there was no point in wishing; you couldn't rewrite history. The question now was: how was she going to persuade him to leave her alone?

She pushed back a windblown lock of red hair, sighing. Tomorrow she would write Larry a formal, very distant letter, asking him to stop ringing and writing. If he didn't take any notice of that she would have to get her solicitor to deal with it.

It was a form of stalking, wasn't it? It made life complicated and she wasn't putting up with any more of it.

If she couldn't persuade him to stop, she would see what the law could do.

The next call on the answer-machine was from another man—but very different; his complaining voice made her laugh. 'Zoe, I'm not happy with the way the budget is shaping…'

'So what's new?' she sarcastically enquired, walking back into the kitchen, leaving the production company accountant fretfully going through a list of production costs so far while she rushed back to stop the soup burning, switched off the heat under the saucepan, set a tray, poured soup into a deep bowl, thinly buttered the toast and carried her meal into the sitting room.

Philip Cross was still talking in his gloomy way as she sat down in her armchair in front of the electric fire.

'Please try to pare down wherever you can, Zoe. The bills for this production are unacceptably high. I'm faxing you a list of suggestions for cutting expenses. The transport costs are ludicrous, for instance—surely you can find cheaper ways of moving stuff? Please ring me when you've read it and let me know your thoughts.'

The answer-machine clicked off and Zoe made a face at it.

'You stuffy little cheese mite! Get back in your biscuit! I'll tell you what I think, all right, but you won't like it!'

She settled down to eat her tomato soup and the fingers of buttered toast, pushing Philip Cross and his economy measures away for the moment. She didn't want to think or start worrying. The heat of the fire was comforting; her weary body was slack and relaxed in the armchair.

When she had finished her meal she lay there for a moment, staring at the red glow of the artificial logs, eyes heavy, yawning widely every so often.

If she didn't move soon she would fall asleep in the chair, and then she would be as stiff as a board in the morning.

Stretching, she made herself get out of the chair. What a day this had been, right up to the last, when that bearded guy had...

Oh, no! She'd forgotten all about him! Zoe looked at her watch and realised half an hour had gone by since she'd got home. Would he still be waiting there? Was there any point in ringing for a taxi for him now?

Well, she had given him her word. She had to keep it. Hurriedly picking up the phone, she dialled the local taxi firm she always used.

A man's voice answered, slow, friendly, with a local burr.

'Hallo, this is Zoe Collins,' she said, and explained about the stranded motorist. 'Could you get someone to drive out and see if he's still there? If he isn't, send me a bill for the call-out.'

'Okay, Miss Collins, we'll deal with it,' the taxi operator said amiably, ringing off.

Zoe turned out the light and carried her tray through to the kitchen, loaded the used crockery in the dishwasher, then went upstairs to have a shower before bed. She had been working flat out all day, both physically and mentally, helping the crew shift heavy equipment, concentrating fiercely on the shoot, walking about, back and forth, trying to watch all her actors, check that they were coping, were giving her everything she wanted for the scene.

It was draining, tough, demanding work. Her body ached and smelt of perspiration. She needed to wash the day's effects off her skin.

She stripped rapidly in her bedroom, then walked into the bathroom and turned on the shower. The warm water was deliciously sensual as it trickled down her back, over her breasts, the flat stomach, her hips, down into the valley between her thighs. Eyes closed, she lifted her damp hair back from her face, arms raised, sighing with pleasure. Now she felt more human. This was one of her favourite moments of the day.

After towelling herself dry she put on warm green brushed cotton pyjamas and was about to slip into bed when she realized she had left her script downstairs. Before she went to sleep she must check her notes on blocking out the scenes she was going to shoot tomorrow. She ran down the stairs and found the script on the kitchen table where she had left it.

Picking it up, Zoe turned to go back upstairs, then froze as she heard a sound outside in the hall. Stiffening, she listened, holding her breath. Floorboards creaked again. Was that the sound of quiet breathing?

The hair bristled on the back of her neck. She hadn't imagined it. There was someone out there.

Hurriedly she looked around for a weapon. The wooden meat hammer? One of the razor-sharp kitchen knives she kept safely sheathed in a cupboard? No, too dangerous—he might take it away from her and use it on her. Her eye fell on the tray she had just used. It was made of varnished wood, was very heavy. Brought down on someone's head, it would knock them out long enough for her to be able to ring the police.

Dropping her script back on the table, she picked up the tray and tiptoed towards the hall just as the handle turned silently and the door began to open. Raising her improvised weapon above her head, Zoe waited, not moving, trying to breathe soundlessly.

As soon as a dark shape loomed up in the doorway she made her move, slamming the tray downwards.

But he must have sensed her presence behind the door, or maybe seen her reflection in the window opposite. At the same instant that she moved, so did he, whirling to grab the tray from her hand as it flashed down towards his head. He threw it across the room to land with a crash that was deafening.

Zoe recognised him a second later, ice trickling down her back. Big, bearded, black-haired...oh, my God, it was the man who had tried to get into her car!

'Don't even try anything,' she gasped, backing, reaching for a chair she could fend him off with. 'I've had self-defence lessons.'

'If you think I'm after your body you're flattering yourself!' His eyes had a derisory glitter that made her face burn.

But she kept her cool, holding the chair between them as a shield. 'What are you after? And how did you get here?'

'Walked. And I'm wetter than ever now, thanks to you.'

'Why is it my fault? I didn't make it rain!'

'You promised to ring for a taxi!'

'I did! Obviously you didn't wait long enough.' She

met the insistent dark eyes and her conscience made her
reluctantly admit the truth. 'Okay, I forgot about you at
first, but then I remembered, and I rang the taxi firm I
always use, and asked them to go and get you.'

'So why didn't they turn up?'

'How do I know? But I did ring them—go on, ring
them and check! They can divert their driver here to pick
you up. The phone's in that room.' She gestured to the
sitting room door. 'Their number is written on the pad
next to it. Be my guest.'

'I intend to be,' he ominously drawled, still smiling,
and her nerve-ends crackled with tension and uneasiness.

'What do you mean by that?'

'I'm soaked to the skin, cold and tired and very hungry. Having walked all the way here in that downpour,
I don't intend to hang around in these wet clothes waiting for a taxi. What I need right now is a hot bath, some
dry, warm clothes and a meal, in that order, and as you
didn't keep your word and send me a taxi right away, I
think you owe it to me to give me what I need.'

'Look, I'm sorry I forgot about your taxi, but I am
not responsible for your problems. I didn't make your
car break down; I didn't make it rain. Stop blaming everything on me! How did you manage to follow me
home, anyway? How did you know I lived here?'

She saw his eyes flicker, a shadow of evasion cross
his face, and her instincts jangled an alarm. What did
that look mean? She suddenly sensed that he knew her,
or of her, at least, and had known just where she lived.
What was going on here? Who was he?

'Are you one of my neighbours?' She knew most of
the nearer neighbours by sight, if not by name, and she

didn't recognise him. If she had ever seen him before she was sure she would remember.

Taking a longer long at him, she thought, Hang on, though! Hadn't she felt at one moment that there was something familiar about him? Zoe tried to hunt the memory down—had she seen him before? And if so, where?

But her mind couldn't come up with anything, except the same uncertain feeling that somewhere, somehow, he was familiar.

'No.' He shrugged. 'I have a flat in London.'

That didn't explain how he had managed to find her cottage or get in, though, so she sharply asked, 'You still haven't told me how you got here, or got inside the cottage!'

He gave her a hostile stare. 'I waited in that torrential downpour for twenty minutes before deciding that you hadn't rung for a taxi for me. I followed you car down this lane because I guessed there must be houses down here and I might be able to get someone to let me use their phone. I saw the lights on in this cottage so I came up the drive, then I recognised your car parked outside. I knocked on the front door three or four times without getting a reply.'

She must have been in the shower, she realised. With the water running and the bathroom door shut she wouldn't have heard him.

'Then I realised the front door was open,' he said.

'That's a lie! I locked it!'

'No, you didn't. It wasn't locked—go and look!' he tersely told her, his dark eyes hard.

She couldn't remember whether or not she had locked

it, actually, but she usually did. She had been in a tearing hurry to get indoors, though.

Absorbing the tired lines in his face, his saturated clothes, in a spasm of reluctant sympathy, she said, 'I can certainly give you some food and a hot drink, but I don't have any men's clothes in my wardrobe. It would be stupid to have a bath and then go out into the rain again. I'll ring the taxi firm, then get you a meal while we're waiting for them—how's that?'

'Hal's right; you are a cold-blooded little vixen!' he said, and she stiffened, eyes narrowing on him.

'Hal?'

'My cousin Hal Thaxford.'

Light dawned. 'Hal Thaxford? You're his cousin?' Her green eyes searched his face, and she finally realised why he had seemed so familiar. Oh, yes, she could see the likeness now—same colouring, same build, same shape of face, even the same frowning glare which had made Hal Thaxford one of the most popular TV stars today. She had a low opinion of Hal's acting ability; he skated along on the surface of his roles, using his looks, his sex appeal, and his usual scowl instead of actually trying to act. Luckily for him, women swooned every time he glowered out of the screen. He got a lot of work and was highly paid, so why should he bother working at his craft?

'Are you an actor?'

'No,' he bit out, white teeth tight. 'I am not. I'm not involved in films in any capacity, but I know all about the tawdry world you live in. Hal has told me all about it—and he's told me all about you, too.'

His hostile eyes ran down over her slender body in

the loose cotton pyjamas which clung to her small, high breasts, flowed over her slim hips and the long, thin legs. She flushed at the mix of sexual assessment and cold derision in that look.

Okay, Hal didn't like her much; it was mutual, she was not one of his fans—but what on earth could he have said to this man to make him eye her like that?

He told her a second later, his voice accusing her, judging her, finding her guilty all at once. 'I know all about the manipulative, heartless games you play with men, flirting with them, letting them fall in love, and then dumping them ruthlessly once you're tired of them. I took his stories with a pinch of salt at the time. I'd seen his photos of you and I couldn't believe any woman who looked the way you do could be such a bitch, but now I've met you, it's obvious Hal didn't exaggerate an inch.'

She was so taken aback that when he walked past her into her sitting room it took her a moment or so to pull herself together and follow him.

'What are you doing?' she began, and stopped as she saw that he had pulled the telephone out of the wall. 'Put that back!'

He whirled and grabbed her arm. 'Come with me,' he muttered, and she dug her heels into the carpet, refusing to move.

'Let me go and get out of my house.'

'I haven't got time to argue with you,' he said, put an arm round her waist and lifted her off the floor as if she was a child.

The breath driven out of her by shock, she gasped,

'Put me down. Put me down! What do you think you're doing?'

Ignoring her, he slung her over his shoulder, her head down his back, her feet drumming against his middle, her arms flailing impotently.

'I'm taking you upstairs,' he coolly informed her as he strode towards the hall, and Zoe felt icy fear trickling down her spine.

CHAPTER TWO

BY THE time he had got upstairs Zoe was recovering from her first shock and able to think clearly. Okay, he was bigger than her, and had a powerful, muscled physique, but she wasn't just giving in or giving up. Her self-respect insisted she fight. As he carried her through the open door of her bedroom she grabbed a large handful of his hair and yanked hard.

'Put me down!'

He dropped her. On the bed. She bounced, out of breath for a second, then, before he could stop her, rolled over to the far side, stood up with her back against the wall and reached for the nearest object she could use as a weapon—a large bronze statuette she had won for one of her TV documentaries years ago; the first award she'd ever been given. She kept it beside her bed, on a shelf on the wall, because winning it had made her so proud she hadn't touched the ground for days. There had been many others since, but none that had given her so much pleasure, and when she was feeling low she still got the same buzz from looking at it.

Now she held it up like a club, meeting his quizzical eyes. 'Don't think I wouldn't use this! It's very heavy. Solid bronze. If I hit you with it, believe me, it will hurt! So keep your distance, Mister, or I'll use it. Don't come any closer than you are now.'

Without answering, he turned towards the door but

not, she discovered, to go out. No, he closed, then locked the door, and slid the key into his pocket.

Zoe's throat dried up. She watched him tensely, gripping the statuette even tighter. 'I meant what I said! Stay away from me or you'll be sorry!'

He began to walk across the room and she barely breathed, her chest hurting, poised for action—but he wasn't heading for the bed; he was going towards the bathroom.

Still without looking at her, he opened the bathroom door, went in and closed the door behind him, then bolted it, while she stared incredulously. A moment later she heard the shower start running, the splashing of water, followed by a deep voice singing a very familiar song she couldn't quite identify. She knew it…what was that?

Feeling ridiculous, standing in the corner holding her bronze statuette up in the air, she put it back in its usual place, climbed back over the bed and hurriedly got dressed again in her oldest pair of jeans and a very long grey sweater she had once borrowed from a guy she was dating. She had forgotten to give it back when she'd told him goodbye. Poor Jimmy. He had been rather like his sweater: long, thin and grey. Grey eyes, brown hair sprinkled with grey, a sad, depressed manner. She couldn't remember why she had ever gone out with him in the first place.

She had only been twenty that year; he had been forty, twice her age, a documentary director with a TV company. His job had impressed the hell out of her, which was why she'd first accepted a date for dinner with him. After that he had pestered, on and on and on, simply

hung around in the corners of her life like a mournful
ghost, occasionally talking her into going to the theatre,
or for a drive to the seaside on a warm Sunday afternoon.

Until she'd realised one day that she could end up
being talked into marriage if she didn't tell him firmly
to go away. Jimmy had told her she had broken his heart,
then he'd drifted sadly away.

Six months later he had married a girl called Fifi
whom he had met on holiday in Paris, city of lovers;
now they had three children, she had heard, and Jimmy
had retired from TV to raise pigs in Normandy.

Hearts mend fast, Zoe thought, her mouth twisting
cynically. They aren't made of glass, they don't shatter,
no matter what people say. Perhaps they were made of
rubber—they certainly bounced.

'Danny Boy'! The name of the song came into her
head at that second. That was what he was singing in
her bathroom! Singing very pleasantly, too—not a professional voice, but it was good to listen to! She had
always loved the old Irish song 'Danny Boy', poignant,
sweet, so familiar she wondered she hadn't recognised
it earlier.

Suddenly she realised he had stopped singing, and the
sound of the shower had stopped too.

What was he doing now? Drying himself, obviously—
her imagination worked overtime on what he would look
like naked; he had a body to die for, she thought, then
pulled a face. Hey, now, stop thinking stuff like that!
Are you asking for trouble?

She heard the bathroom door bolt slip back; the handle
turned, out he came, wearing a black towelling robe
which ended at his knees.

It was hers. He had taken it from the airing cupboard in the bathroom. He was so much bigger and taller than her that it only just met around his waist.

He'd knotted the belt to make sure it didn't fall apart, but the robe was far too short for him. He looked funny. Zoe almost laughed until she realised he was naked under the robe; his long legs still damp, the dark hair clinging flat to his skin, his thin, muscular feet bare. God, he was sexy.

She was disturbed by the intimacy of having him so close to her when he had so little on, and even more disturbed by how it made her feel.

'Put your clothes back on!' she ordered, her skin prickling, and got a cool, level stare which seemed to go right through to her backbone.

'You must be kidding. They're wet and cold. Are you sure you haven't got any men's clothes around? One of your boyfriends didn't leave any here?'

'No, I already told you that!'

'I guess you're the type to chuck their clothes away once you've dumped the guys,' he said derisively.

She resented that, her green eyes flashing. Wait till she saw Hal Thaxford! How dared he spread vicious rumours about her?

'Look here…Mr—what's your name…?'

'Hillier. Connel Hillier,' he said over his shoulder as he began going round the bedroom, opening her wardrobe, rummaging through her chest of drawers.

Unusual name, she thought. Connel. She liked it. 'Well, Mr Hillier…' She stopped, doing a double take as she realised what was happening. 'What on earth do you think you're doing? You've no right to search my room! And there's no point in searching, anyway, you won't find any men's clothes!'

She went over to slam shut the open drawer he was hunting through. 'I said, stop it!'

He straightened, turned, a pair of dark socks in his hand. Zoe wore socks whenever she wore boots to work, which, in winter or wet weather, happened frequently.

'What size are these? Oh, never mind, they're the type that stretch. I should be able to get into them.'

He sat down on her bed, swinging one knee over the other to lift a foot. Zoe looked away as she caught a shadowy glimpse of his thigh. A minute later he stood up, and now he was wearing the socks. 'That's better; my feet were freezing. I hope you've at least got food in the house. I'm starving. Let's go downstairs and get cooking.'

His sheer gall left Zoe speechless, something that rarely happened to her. She hadn't liked him much from the instant she'd set eyes on him; now she was beginning to detest him.

Recovering her breath, she burst out, 'Look, you human steamroller, will you stop pushing me around?'

'Steamrollers flatten people; they don't push them around!'

'Well, you aren't flattening me!'

Ignoring her, he walked into the bathroom and came out carrying his wet clothes in a neat pile. Cool as a cucumber, he produced the key from his trouser pocket and unlocked the bedroom door.

Without looking back to check that she was coming, he vanished, and, discovering that he had left the key in the lock, she almost locked herself in, but on reflection decided that that would leave him free to ransack the rest of the house and make off with half her possessions.

Fuming, she followed him, wondering how on earth she was going to get rid of him. If only her mobile didn't need charging!

Maybe while he was eating she might be able to get to the phone, plug it back in, and ring the police? So long as he didn't hear her and strangle her before the police arrived.

Oh, don't be so melodramatic, she told herself—he isn't the type. If I was casting him I wouldn't make him the murderer. A thug, maybe. A gangster. Somebody to be wary of, that was certain. She'd felt that the minute she saw him in the rainy night, peering into her car. There was something electric, powerful, dangerous about those eyes of his.

By the time she reached the kitchen he was chucking his clothes into her washing machine. He briefly looked at her over his shoulder with those dark, menacing eyes.

'Where's your soap powder?'

She almost said, I'll do it for you, until she caught herself doing it. Female programming! she angrily thought. It's put into us right from childhood—why the hell should I? Let him do his own washing.

'Cupboard next to the machine,' she bit out, and got a dry glance from him. No doubt he had been expecting her to offer to do it for him. Men always expected women to wait on them. That was their own programming. If she ever had a son she would make sure he wasn't brought up to see women as potential servants or toys.

He bent again to open the cupboard and her eyes

flicked round the kitchen in search of possible weapons. A glass rolling pin filled with dried flowers, from Greece, hung on the wall—how about that?

No, that was a souvenir of one of the best holidays she had ever had. She didn't want to break that. One of the saucepans? Not heavy enough. That copper casserole would make quite a dent, though, she thought, gazing at the highly polished dish hanging close to the oven.

The washing machine started and she looked back at him warily. He was now busy inspecting the contents of the fridge and the freezer, taking stuff out and checking the cooking instructions.

'There are plenty of soups,' she offered.

He was reading a pack of microwave chicken curry and shrugged. 'I'm too hungry for soup—this looks good. I see you've got a microwave. I'll have this. Do you want some of it?'

She shuddered at the very idea at this hour. 'No, thanks. I prefer not to eat rich food late at night, and, anyway, I've had some soup. Look, can I ring for a taxi for you now? You can eat your meal while you're waiting.'

He popped the chicken curry into the microwave and punched the numbers at the side. The turntable inside began revolving. 'I shall need my clothes before I leave. I see you've got a tumble dryer. When my things come out of the washing machine I'll put them straight into the dryer.'

Trying not to sound anxious she snapped, 'That will take hours—and you're not staying here after you've eaten your food. I want to ring for a taxi for you.'

He took no notice, opening cupboards again, getting

more stuff out. He looked at the foil-wrapped coffee beans he found, making a face. 'Not brilliant, but I suppose they'll do.'

A little flag of red burnt her cheeks. 'Oh, sorry my coffee doesn't meet your standard. I'll make sure I've got something better next time you break down near my house.'

Her sarcasm was water off a duck's back. He shook some coffee into the electric grinder he had found. 'I like using the traditional, wooden French coffee-grinders,' he told her conversationally. 'You feel you're really getting coffee—nothing else gives you that fresh-ground coffee smell. Instant is a last resort for me!'

'This machine is much quicker and less trouble,' Zoe resentfully told him. 'Like the microwave and the tumble dryer, it does the job in half the time, and saving time is important to me. I'm a career woman, not a house-wife.'

He gave her a sardonic smile as he began to fill the percolator with cold water. 'No cream in your fridge, I see! Dieting, I suppose?' Another of those cool, assessing glances that made her spine shiver. 'Well, I'm not! I'll make do with black coffee, but I hope you've got some sugar.'

'Mr Hillier, I did not invite you to this house, but you are my guest so stop knocking the way I live!' She was really furious now. Who did he think he was? 'There's sugar in the far cupboard on the right.' She looked at her watch. 'Look, I'm exhausted. I've had a tough day and I want to get some sleep before I have to get up again in the morning. Would you please eat your meal and leave? I'm sure the taxi driver won't care what you're wearing.' An idea hit her and she hurried out into the hall, to come back with a long brown drover's mac which she had bought in Australia a couple of years ago.

'You could wear this! Nobody will notice what you're wearing under it.'

He was putting a plate under the oven grill, which he had turned on. He glanced at the coat, came over to take it, held it up against him, nodding. 'Terrific, thanks. At least you've got good taste in clothes. I'll borrow it, but I'll still want to wear my own clothes under it.'

'I'll post them on to you tomorrow.'

Shaking his head, he went over to the microwave as it began to bleep. 'No, I'll wait for them.'

Zoe was almost desperate to get rid of him. Her voice high, she yelled, 'This is my house, and I want you to go!'

He opened the curry and inhaled. 'Smells wonderful.' Switching off the grill, he used a teatowel to get the plate out, tipped the golden chicken and sauce out on to the plate, surrounded it with the fluffy white rice which had also been in the packet, sat down at the table and began to eat with a fork. 'Could you pour the coffee?'

'What did your last slave die of?'

'Delight,' he said, sliding her a wicked glance from under his extraordinarily long black lashes.

Zoe's rage wasn't as strong as her sense of humour; she couldn't help laughing, much though she wished she could.

He grinned at her. 'So you are human?'

'Human—and exhausted,' she told him, pouring coffee into the mugs. She might as well drink some herself—clearly she wasn't going to be able to get rid of him for quite a while, and she couldn't go to bed, leaving a total stranger in her house.

'How many hours did you work today?'

'I was up at five, at work by six,' she told him, sitting down opposite him at the table.

He studied her, brows lifted. 'Your eyes are red. They match your hair.'

Flushed, she crossly snapped, 'Thanks. That makes me feel really glamorous.'

He went on staring at her, his black lashes half down over his eyes. 'The jeans are pretty ancient, aren't they? But you still manage to make them look like high fashion. I'm not sure how. I suppose it's just that you're gorgeous, whatever you wear—even with red eyes! And I must be the millionth man to tell you so. I ought to get a prize for that.' He leaned over and kissed her mouth briefly, a mere brush of his lips, before she could draw back, and then went on coolly eating his chicken curry.

Zoe drew a shaken breath and was furious with herself. Anyone would think she had never been kissed before! That light touch of his mouth had lasted a second or two—she could almost believe she had imagined it except for this odd breathlessness. She rubbed her mouth, glaring. 'You take more liberties than any man I've ever met! What do you do for a living? D'you work in the media? Only reporters have that much gall.'

He laughed. 'No. I'm an explorer.'

She blinked, thinking she'd misheard. 'A what?' Maybe it was because she was so tired that she was feeling so disorientated, her ears and eyes playing tricks on her, her face flushed, as if she had a fever.

'Explorer.' He finished his meal and pushed it away. 'I'm just back from South America. I've been mapping the mountain ranges from Tierra del Fuego all along the coast to the Cord de Mérida, right up in Venezuela. They run from one end of the continent to the other, just inland from the coast, over four thousand miles of mountains, many of them up to four thousand feet high. I've been out there for a year, climbing, filming, drawing.'

Open-mouthed, she asked, 'Alone?' and he laughed, white teeth showing against tanned skin.

'No, thank heavens. I was with an international expedition—Europeans, a couple of dozen of us, all specialists: photographers, a couple of doctors, scientists, geologists, biologists. But we were all climbers; that was essential. In those mountains you need to know what you're doing and you need other people you can rely on. Lives could be lost otherwise.' He yawned, got up, went to the washing machine and bent to look at the contents. 'I'll click this through the cycle now and get it on rinse, then we can pop the clothes into the dryer.'

'You're not married, are you?' Zoe thoughtfully said, watching him deftly adjust the machine.

He turned, gave her a cynical look from those deep, dark eyes, shaking his head. 'No. Don't tell me you have scruples about getting involved with married men? Hal didn't tell me that.'

'Hal doesn't know me as well as he thinks he does!' she broke out angrily. 'He doesn't really know me at all. We've never been what you could call friends!'

'What does that mean? Translate for me. By "friends" do you actually mean lovers?'

'No! I mean what most people mean by the word "friends". Hal and I have worked together...'

'And he never made a pass?' Connel sounded disbelieving, and she could imagine why, knowing Hal Thaxford, who made a pass at any attractive woman he met.

'He made them, yes,' she said coldly.

'And got slapped down?'

'Hard. I told him I wasn't interested, but he wouldn't take no for an answer until I slapped his face too. He isn't very bright, you know, or a very good actor. Too wooden. And typically he thinks he's God's gift. He has no idea he's second-rate. When he finally took on board that I would not get involved with him he started sulking.'

'Hmm.' Connel Hillier was eying her dryly. 'Hal's version of this story is somewhat different. In fact, he says it was the other way round—he wasn't interested in you and you resented it.'

Zoe shrugged, unsurprised. 'Well, you can make your own mind up which of us you believe! And, by the way, I've no intention of getting involved with you, either, Mr Hillier. I asked if you were married because it's obvious you're used to looking after yourself—you know how a washing machine works, and you can do your own cooking. If you were married, your wife would probably do all that.'

'These days most men can take care of themselves, married or not.'

'Some men can! Some men don't see why they should bother, once they're married!'

'A few, maybe. But my brother, for instance, is as

capable of cooking a three-course meal as his wife, because Cherry is a high-powered executive who often
doesn't get home until midnight, so Declan has to take
care of himself when she's busy.'

'They don't have children, presumably?'

He shook his head. 'Cherry's on the fast track at work;
she doesn't plan on having kids for years yet. But she's
only twenty-six; she has plenty of time.'

'And your brother's happy with that?'

'He wants children one day, but he's in no hurry. He
and Cherry only got married a few months ago; they
lead a pretty hectic social life: dinner parties, first nights,
clubbing. They're rarely at home in the evening unless
they're giving a party.'

Zoe was listening intently, but her eyelids were drooping wearily and she couldn't stop yawning, hiding it behind her hand.

The washing machine was going into a spin now.
Connel Hillier took the plastic washing basket down
from the top of the machine, his back to her while he
waited for the washing to come to a halt, but he went
on talking about his brother, his voice low and soft. 'Declan isn't ready for the responsibility of kids yet, anyway. He's far too keen on his social life. I sometimes
wonder why he and Cherry got married at all. They're
both so independent and busy, so involved with their
own lives, they don't seem like a pair, more like flat-
mates. But then who knows what goes on inside a relationship? I often think...'

The quiet murmur of his voice was soothing. It blurred
into the background, became soporific; Zoe yawned, listening to it, couldn't keep her eyes open any longer; she

let them close, her head so heavy on her neck that she slowly bowed it on to her arms on the table in front of her.

She never knew when exactly she fell asleep.

The next she knew was when light flickered across her eyelids. Yawning, she stretched her arms above her head—then realised the light was sunlight. What time was it?

Usually when she woke up it was still dark, even in summer. Film-making began with first light and only ended when the light went. She should have been up hours ago. Sharply turning her head to look at her alarm clock, she saw it was eight o'clock.

Eight o'clock?

Horrified, she sat up—why hadn't the alarm gone off? Surely she couldn't have slept through it?

At the same instant her memory rushed in with images of what had happened last night, and she stiffened, her eyes flashing round the bedroom. How had she got here? For a second or two her head swam with bewilderment.

The last thing she remembered was sitting with her head on her arms, while behind her Connel Hillier talked about his brother.

She must have drifted off to sleep. Yes, but how had she got up here, into bed? Panic flooded her. Her heart beat like a steam hammer in her chest, behind her ribs. She couldn't breathe. What had happened last night? After she fell asleep? She couldn't remember coming upstairs; she hadn't set her alarm. How had she got here?

She had been fully dressed, wearing that old grey sweater and her shabbiest pair of jeans—she lifted the sheet and looked down at herself, turned scarlet. She wasn't wearing them now! All she had on was her bra and panties.

'Oh, my God,' she groaned aloud. He must have carried her up here, stripped her…and then…? What had happened then?

Heat burned in her face. She didn't want to think about it. She flung back the covers and jumped out of bed, grabbed a dressing gown from her wardrobe and put it on, then crept out on to the landing, listening for sounds.

Where was he?

The house was silent; the familiar sounds were all she could hear: a Victorian clock she had bought in a junk shop ticking sonorously from her sitting room, the hum of electricity from the kitchen, and from the trees in the garden a whispering of autumn leaves, the sound of birds.

On tiptoe she went from room to room upstairs, but there was no sign of him, so she stole downstairs and began to search there, but he was nowhere in the house, and nothing seemed to be missing. She didn't have anything very valuable in the way of antiques, of course, but her electrical equipment was all still in place—TV, video player, stereo equipment—none of it had gone.

The kitchen was spotless, the dishes he had used washed up and put away, the sink cleaned, the hob as clean as if he had never been there, and there was no sign of his clothes in the tumble dryer. He must have waited for them to dry properly, then put them on and gone.

Her car! she thought, hurrying to open the front door, but it still stood there, on the drive, where she had left it; the rain was drying on the glossy surface now, the chrome flashing in the sunlight.

She shut the front door again. He had gone, leaving no trace. She might almost have imagined the whole incident. She wished she could believe she had.

But the phone was still unplugged; she hadn't invented him pulling it out of the wall! She bent to plug it back in, then went back upstairs and showered, got dressed, like a zombie, moving automatically in her usual routine before leaving for work, but with brow furrowed, eyes blank in deep thought.

He had carried her upstairs, taken her clothes off and put her into her bed. Was that all he had done?

Had he got in bed with her? Had he...?

No! she told herself fiercely. She would have woken up if he had tried to have sex with her. Of course she would!

She hadn't woken up while he was carrying her upstairs, or taking off her jeans, though. It couldn't have been easy to get her jeans off without disturbing her, could it?

Maybe he had woken her up, though? Maybe she had stirred, becoming aware, woken up? But...if she had, she would remember, wouldn't she? And she didn't recall a thing after she'd put her head on her arms and drifted off to sleep.

She didn't want to think about it. Angrily she ran downstairs, made herself black coffee but didn't eat anything. Her appetite had gone. In fact, she felt sick.

She stood by the window, drinking her hot coffee, staring out at the bright, autumn morning, making herself observe what she saw instead of thinking about last night. In her job that was vital, the act of observing, seeing, far more important than words, and it helped her to forget herself.

After all that torrential rain the sky was blue and cloudless; the sun shone as brilliantly as if it was summer again. Leaves blew across the damp grass of her lawns; orange, bronze, gold, dark brown, they heaped up behind her garden wall. She must get out there and rake them up on her next day off. There were few flowers around now: a bush of dark blood-red fuchsia, the bells drooping, still heavy with yesterday's rain, pale blue and pink lace-capped hydrangeas, a few white winter roses. But autumn had other pleasures; she stared at spiders' webs glittering on bushes, delicate, complex patterns filmed with dew, as bright as diamonds in this sunlight, and fluttering in the wind like ancient flags.

But however hard she tried to think about other things she kept coming back to last night. How was she going to work today? How could she concentrate when somewhere at the edge of her mind was a vague memory, like a dream, half remembered. Warm hands touching her, softly caressing...

Groaning again, she shook her head. No, she didn't remember that. She didn't remember anything.

Her nerves jumped as the telephone began to ring. She slowly went to pick it up, her fingers slippery with perspiration.

'Hello?' She couldn't quite make her voice steady. It wouldn't be him—why should he ring her? Yet somehow she didn't feel she had seen the last of him. He had left her off balance, nervous, with this worrying feeling that something had happened last night that wasn't going to be easy to forget.

'Zoe?' The voice at the other end was uncertain, but very familiar, and she relaxed. 'Is that you? Are you okay?' It was her production runner, Barbara, a lively, eager, hard-working girl in her early twenties, who was normally full of bounce, but this morning sounded faintly anxious.

Pulling herself together, Zoe huskily reassured her. 'Of course I am—what do you mean?'

'You sounded breathless. Did I wake you up? Had you forgotten you called an early start, for five-thirty? Or did you oversleep?'

'Yes, sorry, my alarm didn't go off.' They must all be cursing her, getting them there so early and then not turning up, and she couldn't blame them; she would feel just the same in their shoes. 'I'm just leaving, Barbara. I should be there in half an hour. Has Will started work? Is he setting up the cameras?'

'Yes, he's more or less ready, I think. He just broke to have some breakfast, and there's a crowd of extras milling around eating sausage baps.'

'Okay. I'll get there as soon as I can.'

Zoe hung up, locked the cottage, got behind the wheel of her car and started the engine, pushing away the memory of what had—or hadn't—happened last night.

She would think about that some other time. She couldn't afford to be distracted by anything, or anyone, until this film was finished.

With any luck she would never set eyes on Connel Hillier again, anyway.

CHAPTER THREE

THE following Saturday Zoe wasn't working—she often worked seven days a week, but officially it was six days. The film unions wouldn't permit their members to work all week without a day off, not that that applied to a director, who could work whenever she chose, planning, rewriting, working out shots in a model of the set. Without her film crew, of course. They usually crashed out for hours, so sleep-starved after working long hours every other day that they rarely surfaced again until the evening when they headed for bright lights and some fun.

Zoe got up at eleven that Saturday, had a real breakfast for once, a bowl of fresh fruit and a boiled egg with toast, listening to local radio. Someone had rung her a couple of times without leaving a message on her answer-machine. Who had that been? she wondered, and hoped it hadn't been Larry again. He was becoming a nuisance.

Her sister's voice came on next. 'Aren't you ever at home? Look, tonight, six o'clock, don't forget, or else! Oh, and bring a bottle, preferably red wine. It goes so well with steak.'

After tidying the kitchen and making her bed, Zoe went to the hairdresser, then ate lunch in the local pub, which did a wonderful mushroom risotto, played a concentrated game of dominoes with friends. At two-thirty she drove to the local supermarket and did her weekend shopping, then went home to put it all away before doing an hour's housework. She enjoyed Saturday; it was peaceful and restful not to have to tell anyone else what to do, and to be able to sleep as late as she liked and be as lazy as she chose.

At four she stripped down to her bra and panties and went back to bed for an hour, setting her alarm to make sure she woke up in time to go to her sister's barbecue.

The alarm going off was a shock to her system. She was dragged out of a dream, her nerves jangling, but that was normal to her. Eyes still shut, she groped her way to the clock, to push down the button, then swung her legs out of bed to make sure she didn't fall asleep again.

Yawning and flushed, she stretched, stood up, opened her eyes and made her way to the bathroom to shower before getting dressed. The lukewarm water was refreshing, cooling down her skin, waking her properly. Standing by the window later, she saw that the wind and rain had passed. The weather had warmed up, the late-evening sun was shining, the sky was blue and clear, not a cloud in sight. It could be summer instead of autumn. A perfect evening for a barbecue.

She put on her favourite casual outfit, a jade-green trouser suit. Under the jacket she wore a bronze silk sleeveless tunic so fine it could be drawn through the exactly matching bronze Celtic bracelet she wore on one arm. She had bought this replica at the British Museum shop; it was inscribed with runic writing.

It was nearly six-thirty by the time she got to her sister's house and the barbecue was already crowded and noisy, mostly with children, Zoe was sorry to see. Her nephews rushed at her, pink and excited.

'A balloon landed on the barbie and blew up!'

'Dad went crazy!'

'You should have heard him shouting!'

They both giggled, looking at each other. 'It really made him jump!'

Zoe eyed them shrewdly. 'It wouldn't have been you two who lobbed the balloon on to the barbie, by any chance?'

'Us?' The eldest, seven-year-old Felix, said innocently, his eyes reminding her of his father. You could see already what Felix would look like when he was Mark's age—he was going to be tall, dark, bony, very attractive.

'It just blew down from a tree, honestly!' six-year-old Charlie said, but a dimple in his cheek and a chuckle in his voice gave him away. He wasn't yet quite out of babyhood, face and body still soft and downy, but he tumbled in his big brother's wake everywhere, falling over, bruising himself, but determined to do everything Felix did. He wasn't as much like his father. Zoe saw her sister in him, Sancha's warmth, her tenderness, her sensitivity. No need to worry about Felix; he was as tough as a tree and full of confidence. But Charlie was different. Zoe knew Sancha worried about him.

'Oh, there you are! I said six, not half past!' Sancha gave her a quick hug, then looked her up and down, making a face. 'You look as if you're dressed for a nightclub. I suppose you bought that outfit in Paris when you went there last month?'

'No, London, and it's a year old! Sorry I'm late. I had

so much to do. My one day off! I've been rushing about, shopping, doing housework. Here, my contribution to the bar!' Zoe handed her sister the two bottles of red Chianti she was carrying.

'Chianti! Lovely. Thanks. It will remind us of our wonderful Tuscan holiday—it was quite a wrench to come back. We loved it, didn't we, boys?'

'Yeah,' Charlie said blissfully. 'I drank lots of wine.'

'You had a sip from your father's glass once or twice!' Sancha rephrased, smiling indulgently.

'It was really cool!' Felix said nostalgically. 'We had a pool and swam every day. I taught Flora to swim.'

'To float, anyway.' His mother nodded. 'She looked so sweet, paddling around in a plastic duck boat. Did I show you the photos, Zoe? I must get them out later.'

'I can't wait. Talking of monsters, where is she?' Zoe looked around warily.

At once alarmed, Sancha looked around too. 'Boys, where is she? I told you to look after her.'

'Under that bush,' Charlie told her, pointing a stubby pink finger at a blue hydrangea covered in great, lacy heads of sky-blue flowers. Flora, in pink dungarees and a pink sweater, her red hair tousled and stuck with several of the bright blue flower-heads, lay on her back under the branches, fast asleep, her mouth open, snoring loudly, a piece of doughnut clutched in one hand.

Sancha's face glowed with mother love. 'Doesn't she look adorable?'

'That's not a word I'd ever apply to Flora, but that's how I like her best, fast asleep and not doing anything,' Zoe admitted. 'It's when she wakes up and starts getting about that I get nervous.'

The boys grinned. 'Me, too,' Charlie agreed.

'She always wants to play with us,' Felix complained. 'And she's too little and keeps falling over, and screaming, then we get blamed.'

'You're the oldest; you should take care of your baby sister,' their mother scolded, and the boys grimaced at their aunt.

From the barbecue site Mark waved, calling, 'Come and help, boys!'

'We have to be waiters,' Felix gloomily said. 'And give out the food to people. It's boring.'

'Off you go,' their mother insisted, however, so they trudged off reluctantly, as if there was lead in their shoes.

'So what's the great news you mentioned?' Zoe asked her sister, and Sancha beamed.

'I'm going to start my own firm!'

Amazed, Zoe asked, 'Doing what?'

'Photography, stupid! I've taken a lease on a shop in Abbot Street, just behind the High Street. It will take a couple of months to make some essential changes to the shop fittings, so I'll open up around Christmas, specialising in children and make-overs.'

'Make-overs?'

'Oh, you know—a woman comes in wanting a photo that makes her look better than she usually does! Martha is going to do the hair and make-up; we're going into partnership. When she's transformed the client I take a series of soft-focus shots.'

'You should make millions,' Zoe said, laughing.

'You may laugh. You don't need a helping hand—some women do! I did myself a year ago, remember.'

'Well, you don't need one now; you look terrific!' Zoe said, smiling at her. 'And I'll keep my fingers crossed your new venture is a huge success. Is Mark okay about it?'

'Very supportive—in fact, he put up half the money. He insisted. He thinks I've had a brilliant idea and he wanted to back me. Mark's very shrewd, too, so it was very encouraging to know he approved of my concept.'

'Amazing,' Zoe murmured. 'The man surprises me sometimes. But then all men give you surprises, not all of them pleasant.'

'Talking about men, where's yours?' asked Sancha.

'Who?' Zoe stared at her in bafflement.

'Whoever you're seeing at the moment—I told you to bring a guy.'

Zoe shrugged. 'I'm not seeing anyone. I'm too busy for a social life.'

'What happened to…was it…Harry? No, Larry? He was the last one I met.'

'He turned out to be a bit weird, so I broke it off.'

Sighing heavily, Sancha told her, 'Zoe, if you keep dumping men like this you'll end up a lonely spinster!'

'I've heard that a hundred times! And I'm not lonely, nor do I spin. Or sew, come to that. Women don't have to marry these days to enjoy life. I've got a career that's more important to me than any man I ever meet. I earn a lot of money and have a lot of fun, and above all I love my work. I enjoy men's company when I'm in the mood but I don't need a man to make my life complete.'

'One day you'll want children, Zoe! Don't leave it too late.'

'You mean a brat like Flora?' Zoe said scathingly. 'Do me a favour! I'd rather have a cat!'

'You don't mean that!'

'Oh, yes, I do! You can put a cat out at night and it amuses itself. They're clean, too. Kids are far more trouble and make far more noise and mess. I won't pine if I never have one. Come on, open this wine and pour me a glass, then I'll get some food out of Mark. I can smell steak and onions cooking—and I'm starving!'

When she walked over to the barbecue, a glass of red wine in her hand, flame-red hair ruffled by the evening breeze, startlingly vivid in the jade-green suit, Mark raised his brows at her in that macho, sardonic way that made her teeth meet.

'No man tonight, Zoe?'

She glanced over the loaded barbecue. 'Have you got one ready to eat?'

'Well, I had heard the rumours that you eat men for dinner, but I didn't realise it was true!' Mark said dryly. 'Sorry, we're just serving steak, lamb chops, gammon chops or sausages.'

'Steak will do, then—and some of those onions, please, the ones that haven't burnt black yet.'

'No criticisms of my cooking, please!' Mark's lean body bent to scoop up the food while she watched him critically. She wasn't Mark's type any more than he was hers. She found his manner to her sister far too overbearing. Why did Sancha put up with it?

Everything about him was too much—he was too tall, too powerful, too energetic, too demanding, too masculine, had too much ego, was too good-looking. He made Zoe's hackles rise as soon as she set eyes on him, and she knew he had the same reaction to her. Mark preferred his women ultra-feminine: soft, gentle, warm and tender, preferably submissive. Sancha fitted the bill exactly.

A year ago they had gone through a bad patch and Zoe had thought for a while there would be a divorce and her sister might get a life at last, but they had somehow worked out all their problems, and she had to admit that they seemed happy together now. Their lives had changed considerably since Mark got a new job; he didn't earn as much but he had more time off, and Sancha said he enjoyed his work more. He had had to spend most of his time in an office in his last job—with this one he spent a lot of time on site. A civil engineering company, his new firm were building a bypass around an ancient town so choked with traffic as to be a nightmare both for the people who lived there and anyone visiting it, and Mark could drive home in half an hour. He saw far more of Sancha and the children and had plenty of time off to spend at home.

All of which made it astonishing that he was backing Sancha in her new project, but then Flora went to playschool every morning now she was three, which meant that Sancha could work part-time without interfering with Mark's life, especially if Martha was going to help in the shop. One of them could pick Flora up from school and take her back to the shop each day. Being able to get away from Flora for a few hours had put the life back into Sancha's brown eyes. She no longer looked exhausted, thank heavens; she was vibrant and cheerful whenever Zoe saw her now.

Having her own business and being able to give free

rein to her creativity and common sense would make her even happier.

'Help yourself to salad.' Mark gestured, handing her a plate with her steak and a heap of fried onions on it.

As she turned Zoe bumped into a man waiting behind her, automatically muttering, 'Sorry,' although it was really his fault for standing so close.

'That's okay, I'm getting used to you knocking me about!'

The deep voice made her start and look up in amazement. For a second or two she stared blankly, until she suddenly recognised Connel Hillier, now minus his black beard, clean-shaven, his hair brushed back from his hard-featured face, showing her that he was far better looking than she had realised. It was a strong, tenacious face, with high cheekbones and a wide setting to those liquid dark eyes, his mouth wide and beautifully shaped.

'What are you doing here?' Zoe demanded, scowling. He was wearing skin-tight dark blue jeans and a black shirt which lay open at his tanned throat, tie-less, making you immediately conscious of his masculinity, the wide shoulders, slim waist, lean hips and long legs. He certainly wasn't a wallpaper person, she thought, watching him with hostile eyes.

'I invited him,' Mark said. 'Do you two know each other? I had no idea.'

'No,' Zoe denied.

'Yes,' Connel said.

Mark looked from one to the other with a coolly curious expression. 'Which of you is lying, I wonder?'

'Which do you think?' Connel grinned at him. 'Women always lie at the drop of a hat.'

'We don't *know* each other!' Zoe snapped. 'We simply met. Once. And once was enough for me. How on earth do you know him, Mark? I thought he'd been out of the country on some sort of exploring trip for years.'

'He's my boss,' said Mark, and her mouth opened in a gasp.

'Your boss? He can't be! He told me he was an explorer!' She turned on Connel, bristling. 'You lied to me!'

'No, I didn't. I have spent the last year with an international expedition to South America, exploring the mountain ranges. But I'm also managing director of a civil engineering firm. I took a sabbatical while my father ran the business for a year.'

Her mind ticked busily, remembering things he had said to her the night they met.

'And you said you lived in London!'

'I have a flat in London—I inherited it from an aunt and haven't got around to selling it yet.'

He'd claimed to have heard about her from Hal Thaxford, but maybe Mark had talked about her, too. What had Mark said about her?

She looked at her brother-in-law suspiciously. Mark had an amused look now. 'Your food must be getting cold—get some salad and eat your meal before it's ruined, Zoe!'

'I'll talk to you later,' she threatened him, and turned to grab a pile of salad, then went to find her sister, who was sitting on the grass talking to a neighbour, Martha Adams.

Sprawling beside them, Zoe said, 'Hi, Martha—how

are you? You look terrific in that outfit; red really suits you.'

'Thanks. You look great, yourself; I love the suit.' Marsha smiled. Barely five foot, she was as slim as a girl, despite being in her early forties. 'Bet I can guess who made it,' she added, naming a world-famous designer.

'I'm impressed—you're absolutely right. You've got a good eye!'

'I just remember when you bought it,' confessed Martha.

'Cost me an arm and a leg!'

'It was worth it. I love the cut, only wish I could afford it.'

'It's a classic design—I've had it for a year and I shall wear it until it falls to pieces. The style won't go out of fashion, so it was worth the money. But your red jeans are beautifully cut, too.'

Martha gave her a delighted smile. 'I made them myself.'

'You're kidding!' Zoe slowly examined the older woman's clothes. 'Did you make the grey shirt, too?'

'No, that was a Christmas present, from Sancha and Mark! I love your brown top, by the way—it's so sleek and yet it almost glitters like gold.'

'It's not brown; it's bronze,' corrected Zoe. 'Yes, I love it, too. I hope that will last for years, too.' She glanced at her sister. 'How long have you known Connel Hillier?'

'I don't know him at all. He's the head of Mark's new firm.' Sancha stared curiously. 'Do you know him? You never mentioned him. Don't tell me he's your new guy? That's amazing!'

'He's nothing of the kind! I only met him once, and it wasn't a pleasant experience. Remember that terrible storm we had earlier this week? I was driving home after a very long day filming, and while I was waiting at the crossroads to turn down my lane he tried to get into my car.'

'What do you mean?' Startled, Sancha and Martha both watched her incredulously.

'Tried to get into your car?' Martha asked.

In between eating mouthfuls of her food, Zoe told them what had happened that night, and they listened open-mouthed.

'He actually broke into your cottage?' asked Sancha in disbelief.

'Yes, I was just about to get into bed when I heard him creeping about downstairs.'

Martha murmured, 'Seeing you here tonight must have been a big shock for him!'

'He didn't turn a hair! The way he acted you'd have thought we were old pals. He actually made fun of me for being offhand with him.'

Sancha said uneasily, 'The trouble is, Zo, Mark loves his new job. I don't know if he would tell him to go!'

'Tell who to go?' enquired Mark, and they all looked round at him as he joined them with a plate of food and curled his tall frame up on the grass beside them.

'Connel Hillier!' Sancha said anxiously. 'I know you think he's a great guy, but wait till you hear what he did to Zoe! Zoe, tell Mark what you just told us.'

Zoe looked past Mark at Connel Hillier, who had just

strolled up, a glass in his hand, and was eying her with sardonic amusement.

'Yes, do tell us, Zoe,' he drawled.

'You've got a nerve!' she snapped at him, her hands screwing into fists. 'Coming here, laughing at me, after what you did to me!'

'I'm still waiting to hear exactly what he did do!' Mark said, fork poised to put steak into his mouth, and clearly not at all worried by the threatened disclosures.

Darkly flushed under Connel's mocking gaze, she snapped, 'He broke into my cottage…'

'I walked in after ringing the bell; the front door was unlocked.'

'You picked me up and carried me forcibly upstairs! Then locked me into my own bedroom!'

Mark whistled. 'I have to agree, Con, you do have a nerve. Not many men would be brave enough to take such a risk.'

Other guests drifted closer, eavesdropping in fascination, but Connel Hillier seemed untroubled by the scene he was causing. His voice casual, he said, 'You forced me to manhandle you by being unreasonable. I would never have done it otherwise. You tried to make me leave when it was really all your fault that I was freezing and soaked to the skin. Have you told your sister that? Did you tell her how long you left me standing in that storm, waiting for a taxi you never sent?'

'I did ring for one!'

'An hour later!'

'Half an hour later, maybe,' she reluctantly admitted.

'While I stood there getting wetter and wetter. I might have caught pneumonia. I had to get my saturated clothes off at once, and have a hot shower. It was a question of survival.' He looked piteously at Sancha, whose face was concerned. Zoe regarded her sister irritably. Sancha was always being sorry for people!

Connel added, 'And I cooked my own meal.'

Sancha looked at Zoe reprovingly. 'You should have done that for him in those circumstances, Zo!'

Before Zoe could retort, Connel added with a sigh, 'And I washed my clothes, myself. I didn't ask you to do anything for me, did I? And when you fell asleep while I was eating my supper I...'

'Oh, shut up!' she shouted, having left out the final instalment of the story when she told her sister and Martha what had happened.

'She fell asleep?' asked Mark, eyes bright.

'At the table!' Connel nodded.

'So what did you do then?'

'I'm a gentleman. What else could I do but carry her upstairs?'

'Absolutely,' agreed Mark solemnly. 'And then what did you do?'

Before Connel could reply Zoe got to her feet. 'I want to talk to you!' she said to him through her teeth, face hot, and stalked away, hearing Mark laughing behind her. She and her brother-in-law had very little in common—or maybe far too much?

They were both determined and confident, both exercised authority without losing sleep over it. Telling people what to do didn't worry either of them. But they had never got on. She disapproved of the way Mark treated her sister; he disliked almost all her attitudes to life, the universe, everything, but particularly towards his own sex. Mark expected respectful submission—and he had never got it from her!

'Where are you taking me?' Connel murmured, catching up with her. 'Somewhere private? How about your cottage? Preferably your bedroom. I liked it in there. I had fun.'

They were out of view of the rest of the party by then, behind a row of young Leyland cypress which Mark had planted when he laid out this garden, to screen the garbage bins and a shed, and which were busily shooting up skywards although they were only a few years old.

Turning on Connel, Zoe coldly said, 'What exactly have you told my brother-in-law?'

'Not a syllable,' he drawled, looking down at her from his greater height with gleaming, narrowed eyes. 'He only knows what you told him.'

She didn't believe him. 'Then how come he kept laughing like that?'

'I guess he found you funny. Doesn't everybody? Let me give you a tiny piece of advice. If you don't want people to be curious, don't make them suspect you're trying to hide something.'

She froze on the spot. 'What am I supposed to be hiding?'

'You tell me.' But he watched her with those mocking eyes and her colour rose even higher.

'I don't know! And you know I don't know. But you know...'

'No, I don't know,' he said, grinning. 'What exactly do you suspect I know? Or is it as plain as the nose on my face?'

Infuriated, she muttered, 'Stop playing on words—I'm in no mood for your games!'

'Oh, but I'm having so much fun. Don't you like playing games, Zoe?' His tone was soft, seductive, disturbing. She refused to let it get to her.

'No, I do not! And stop changing the subject.'

'I wasn't. Isn't that what we're talking about?'

'We're talking about what you did after I fell asleep!'

'As I just told Mark, what else could I do but carry you up to bed?'

'You didn't tell him you took my clothes off!' she hissed.

He smiled beatifically, his gaze wandering down over every inch of her with what she was afraid was enjoyable nostalgia. 'I hadn't forgotten, believe me.'

That was what she was afraid of.

'You didn't mention that, either, I noticed,' he observed, still watching her closely.

She didn't answer, her lips tight.

'Embarrassed about it?' he enquired. 'I'd never have expected you to be bothered by a man taking your clothes off.'

'You…you…h-had no right!' she stammered, almost incoherent with rage.

'Well,' he said in a pretence of reasonableness, 'I couldn't let you sleep in your clothes, could I?'

She swallowed before asking icily, 'And…and then…what?'

Face as calm as a glass of milk, he enquired, 'How do you mean?'

Her eyes hated him. 'You know what I mean. After you took off my clothes…'

'You must have been having a lovely dream,' he purred, sensuality in those dark eyes.

'Dream?' She had had a dream—but how could he have known that? Unless...unless it hadn't been a dream, and she really had felt those stroking, coaxing hands on her. If only she knew for certain! she thought in confusion. It was not knowing that was the problem.

He watched her betraying face like a cat at a mouse-hole. 'You look as if you're remembering now.'

Skin hot enough to burst into flames, she snarled, 'Stop insinuating and tell me! What did you do after you'd taken my clothes off?'

He leaned down towards her, his powerful body a mixture of intimacy and what she perceived as threat. Keeping her chin lifted, her eyes defied him.

'What did you dream I did?' he whispered, and the hairs on the back of her neck prickled.

'What makes you think you show up in my dreams?'

He put out a long finger and she stiffened as his cool skin stroked her cheek, trickled slowly down to her throat. That was what it had felt like in her dream, those strong, desiring hands touching her. Her stomach seemed to drop out of her.

'If I don't now, I will, Zoe,' he murmured, and she angrily knocked his hand away.

'Don't touch me.'

'I already have. And I will again,' he promised softly, and her mouth went dry.

'Oh, no, you won't!' she threw back, and was furious with herself because her voice shook.

He came a couple of steps closer. 'Oh, yes, I will, Zoe.'

She knew he was laughing at her, but something else was far more worrying. Their bodies were too close. Almost touching. A frantic pulse began beating in her neck. She knew what was happening to her. She wasn't a schoolgirl. At thirty-two she was experienced enough to recognise all the reactions of her body. She knew what it meant, the fierce pumping of blood around her veins, the breathlessness, the heat between her thighs. She might hate the sight of Connel Hillier, but she couldn't deny he got to her sexually. His body spoke to hers below the level of consciousness. She knew she wanted him. The violence of her response was growing, her intelligence drowned by the primitive nature of what was happening inside her. How stupid can you get? she wildly asked herself. He's the last man on earth you should even think about.

Except that thinking didn't come into it. What she felt had nothing whatever to do with her brain. It was all physical. Chemical. Breathing thickly, she found that admission comforting—how could you do anything about your own chemistry?

She stared up at him, a deep-seated ache of desire churning in her stomach. Silence engulfed them both. Connel watched her back. She heard him breathing thickly, rapidly, and felt the heat of his body intensifying. He wanted her, too. Strange how, without a word said on either side, they both knew how they felt. Body language, she thought. Our bodies speak to each other without our volition.

His head slowly lowered; she watched his mouth come closer. Her lips parted, her eyes began to close.

Then small hands fastened round her leg, making her

jump sky-high. Her eyes fluttered open; she looked down in shock.

'Oh, it's that brat,' Connel groaned as they both saw Flora, pink-faced, bright-eyed.

Still clutching Zoe's leg, she demanded, 'What you doing, Aunty? Playing? Don't like that game—let's play hide and seek. Me, too. Want play hide and seek. Now.'

'Three's a crowd,' Connel dryly said. 'I'll go and have a chat with her father. Taking care of Flora is women's work.'

'Coward,' she flung after him as he walked away. He simply laughed.

'Play hide and seek, play hide and seek,' yelled Flora, glaring up at her.

Zoe capitulated. They played hide and seek around the row of young cypress trees for ten minutes before she managed to persuade Flora to return to her mother. Sancha and Martha were in the kitchen washing up glasses when Zoe found them.

'Here's your little ray of sunshine back. I can't take any more,' Zoe told her sister, and Flora ran to hug her mother and lean on her in the confiding way of small children who feel utterly certain of being loved.

'Mumma! Aunty Zoe's mean...she was playing games with Uncle Con, but now she won't play with me!'

The two women gazed at Zoe's pink face with sharp-eyed interest.

Crossly, she complained, 'I played hide and seek with her for ages!'

Sancha grinned. 'She's crotchety because it's long past her bedtime.'

'I'll take her up,' Martha readily said, scooping the toddler up and carrying her out. They heard her crooning a lullaby as she went. 'Sleepy Flora, Sleepy Flora, up the wooden hills to Bedfordshire…'

Flora's voice answered between yawns. 'Don't want…go bed…no…want go back to party…'

'Martha actually seems to enjoy looking after her; she must be half-witted,' Zoe said, wondering how to get away without being too obvious about it before her sister started asking the questions she could see burning on Sancha's tongue.

'She hasn't got any children, and she loves Flora,' Sancha absently said, starting fixedly at her sister.

Zoe looked at her watch and pretended to start in amazement. 'Good heavens, look at the time—I must go; I have to be up at five tomorrow.'

Ignoring that, Sancha demanded, 'Where did you and Connel Hillier vanish to? What's going on, Zo?'

'We were arguing,' Zoe said, rewriting the scene a little.

'What did Flora mean about you two playing games?'

'Who knows?' Zoe couldn't meet Sancha's eyes. Her sister knew her too well; she could read her expressions and Zoe did not want her to do so this time.

'What games?'

'Ask Flora. She was the one who said it. Got to go, Sancha. Lovely party. See you soon.'

'Leave Connel alone,' her sister yelled after her. 'I know what happens to men you dump. They can turn nasty. I don't want Mark losing his job just because you couldn't keep your claws out of his boss!'

'I wouldn't touch his boss with a bargepole!' Zoe

said, slamming out of the kitchen. Typical. Connel Hillier makes a pass at her, despite having it made crystal-clear that she isn't interested in him, and her own sister assumes she was the one doing the chasing.

It took her several minutes to edge her car out of the crowd of others parked along the lane. She had only drunk a couple of glasses of wine, but the incident with Connel and then the clash with her sister had made her agitated and prone to clumsiness. She inched back and forth a number of times before finally getting out of the space.

She was ten minutes from her home when she heard a loud bang and felt a sharp drag on the steering wheel. Startled, she slowed her speed, but the car was out of control, sliding sideways across the road, making a strange slapping noise which she suddenly recognised as a burst tyre. She must have run over something sharp, a nail or broken glass.

Braking hard, she fought to regain control, but was unable to stop the car heading down into the ditch on the far side of the road.

Luckily, there was a grassy bank on the other side of the ditch, rather than a wall. Her car bonnet crashed into it, the metal crumpling like paper. She was flung violently forwards into the airbag, which had exploded out into the car from behind her wheel.

Thank heavens for airbags, thought Zoe, before passing out.

CHAPTER FOUR

'ZOE? Zoe. Wake up. Can you hear me?' The voice was familiar and she stirred, wincing at the pain her movement caused.

Someone close beside her sighed with relief. 'Thank God for that. I thought you might be out of it.'

'Go away,' she said without opening her eyes, feeling the pillow underneath her face giving, almost billowing around her. Who was that? What was he doing in her bedroom? At some level of her mind she knew, but she couldn't put a name to the voice even though she recognised it. 'I'm very sleepy. Leave me alone.'

'Stay awake. You've got to get out of there; I can smell petrol,' the voice ordered, and she prickled with resentment over the note of authority. Who did he think he was?

'Shut up,' she groaned.

His voice became urgent. 'Don't go back to sleep—Zoe, listen to me—the doors are jammed; I can't get you out out unless you wake up. Can you reach your seat belt and undo it? The windscreen has gone. I'll get you out through there easily enough once you've taken off your seat belt.'

'Seat belt?' she said, dazedly. What did he mean, seat belt? Wasn't she in bed? With the utmost reluctance she forced her eyes open and realised that the pillow her head was nestling against was actually an inflated white airbag. She sat up, grunting in pain as her ribs and neck hurt.

'What happened?' she asked, absorbing the sight of broken shards of glass littering the car bonnet and the seats around her, the angle at which the car was buried in the ditch, the crumpled bonnet from which a grey smoke filtered. For some reason there were bright lights illuminating the scene, although this was a dark country road. 'I crashed. I crashed the car!' she thought aloud.

'Never mind that. Stop chatting. Get out of there now, Zoe!'

Panic set in and she scrabbled at her seat belt. 'It won't open, it won't...'

'Keep calm. Stop for a second, take a deep breath...don't panic, Zoe.'

'I'm not panicking!' But she knew she was, so she obeyed him, breathing deeply, trying to clear her head before she had another go at the seat belt.

This time it clicked and she was free.

'Out you come!' the man leaning in through the gaping frame of the windscreen said, his hands held out to her.

She looked up into his face, groaning. 'You!' But hadn't she recognised Connel Hillier's deep, male voice all along? She simply hadn't wanted to think about him.

His mouth twisted. 'Who did you think it was? Come on, there's no time to waste. You have to get out of there.'

She took his hands, flinching at the pain his grip caused her. She must have cuts all over her own hands, she realised, and no doubt there were bits of glass in the cuts. Her ribs hurt too. In fact, she was bruised from head to foot.

He pulled her up towards him. She gave a cry of pain as she emerged from the windscreen. A second later she was over his shoulder, her head hanging dizzily down the other side, and he was carrying her away from the smoking car towards the bright lights she had noticed a moment ago, and which turned out to be the headlights of Connel's car.

He slid her into the front passenger seat and rapidly belted her in, closed the door on her and ran round the other side. Zoe was too disorientated to resent the way he was manhandling and ordering her around. Dazedly she stared in horror at her smashed car. My God, she'd been lucky to get out of that alive. It was a write-off! Well, her insurance would pay for a new car, but that would mean that her insurance costs were going to soar next year. It was maddening because she had never had an accident before, and had been getting excellent no-claim bonuses for years.

Connel climbed in next to her hurriedly and without a word started the engine and drove off at speed round a bend in the road where he slowed and stopped in a lay-by.

Zoe looked suspiciously at him. 'What do you think you're doing?'

He ignored her, staring into his wing mirror.

'Why have you stopped?' she began, just as there was a violent explosion and the road behind them was lit up by flames.

Connel whistled. 'I knew it! We only just got out of range in time!'

'Th...that was my car,' she whispered, starting to shake, her eyes fixed rigidly on the wing mirror in which she could see the flames.

Connel leaned down and produced a mobile phone from the floor of his seat, began talking into it. Zoe didn't take much notice; she was too busy watching the flames climbing into the sky, realising how narrowly she had missed being killed.

'Are you okay?'

She started, looking at Connel dazedly as he replaced his phone. 'What?'

Patiently he asked, 'How do you feel?'

'How do you think I feel?' she muttered. 'I just crashed my car, I'm aching from head to foot, I nearly died—how would *you* feel if you were me?'

He brushed her tangled hair back from her pale face. 'Okay, calm down.' Leaning over, he produced a thick tartan car rug from the back seat and folded it over her, tucked it in under her chin and down the side of her body. 'I just rang the police to report the accident. The fire brigade will be along soon, but the desk sergeant said I could take you off to hospital without waiting for them to arrive. They'll talk to you later, when you've had medical treatment.'

'I don't want to go to hospital! I'm not badly injured,' she said in a high, shaking voice. 'I just want to go home to my own bed.'

In the same calm, soothing voice, Connel said, 'You should have an X-ray as soon as possible. You were out cold when I arrived, but I wasn't far behind you. I left soon after you did, so it may not be serious. In case you have concussion, though, you must be checked by a doctor. You're obviously in shock and you may need medication.'

'I'm fine! Just take me home, will you?'

His dark eyes probed her face. 'Look in the mirror. You're as white as a ghost.' He started the car. 'I've put the seat-warmer on for you, and turned the heating up high. You'll start to feel better as soon as you're warmer.'

Zoe closed her eyes and sulked. Why did it have to be Connel Hillier who found her? He was the last man in the universe she would want to see her in this condition. She had never felt this weird before and it scared her. What was wrong with her? Was he right? Did she have concussion? Or was this simply shock?

The car was doing a speed that made her heart stop. She had never been bothered by fast driving before, but suddenly she was terrified.

'You're driving too fast!'

His voice seemed to come from far away. 'We have to get you to hospital as soon as possible. Shock can be dangerous.'

'W...w...who s...said I w...was in ssshhh...shock?' she managed, despite her chattering teeth. 'I...I'm j...j...just c...c...cold. And stop driving so fast!'

'Okay, I will. Don't get upset, just lie back and keep warm,' Connel soothed.

The car slowed and she closed her eyes again. The rug was warm, and she could feel the car heating building up, but she was still shivering as Connel drove into the nearest town, some quarter of an hour later. Zoe heard the noise of traffic, sensed that they were out of the country and into busy streets, but she didn't want to open her eyes even when they turned off the road and slowed to a stop.

Connel got out and came round to help her out, but her legs had become rubbery. They gave under her, and Connel picked her up into his arms and carried her inside the building. Her head lolling on his chest, she drifted in and out of awareness, but she knew they were in a hospital by the smell—disinfectant, polish, flowers.

The next couple of hours passed in a sort of daze. She had an X-ray, saw a doctor, had lights shone in her eyes, was examined from head to toe, and told she had a seat belt burn across her body, but she was very lucky the belt had not given way or she might have been killed.

The tired young Casualty doctor smiled at her. 'The cuts and bruises aren't a problem; they'll heal quite quickly. In a few days you won't know they were there. I don't think you have concussion. There are no signs of internal injury in the X-rays, or fractures or brain damage. We don't need to keep you in overnight, but if you get headaches, or problems with your eyes, come back at once. They will be a sign that you may have a problem. When you get home, go straight to bed, take some pills I'm going to give you, and rest for a few days. You're in mild shock, but it doesn't seem serious to me. Your friend will take care of you, will he?'

Friend? she thought vaguely, but nodded, not sure who he meant.

'I'm just going to give you an injection,' the doctor added, and Zoe jumped as he stuck a needle into one of her arms. 'Did that sting? Sorry about that,' he cheerfully said.

'You need to go back to medical school and get some

more training,' she muttered, and he laughed as if she had intended to be funny.

She hadn't.

When he showed her out of his consulting room she realised which "friend" he had been talking about as she saw Connel, who sat outside, reading a newspaper.

'Everything okay?' he asked, getting up. 'I've managed to find a wheelchair—you aren't really heavy, but carrying you about like this is seriously damaging my muscles.'

The doctor laughed.

Zoe's teeth grated. 'I can walk. I'm not a cripple.'

'Nonsense,' both men said together, and between them lifted her into the wheelchair. Her dignity would not let her struggle. Connel wrapped his tartan rug round her again, as if she was a baby, then he moved away a little and stood talking to the doctor in tones too low for her to hear what was being said, not that she cared. She was yawning, and dying to go to sleep.

Connel seized the wheelchair a moment later and began pushing her through the long, dull corridors. There was a surreal feeling to the place, to her mood; she half believed she was already asleep and dreaming.

Afterwards she never remembered Connel putting her back into his car. She slept throughout the journey home to her cottage, slept as he picked her up, still wrapped in her rug, and carried her up the stairs to her bedroom.

Only as he put her down on her bed did she surface, briefly, to stare up into his face, confused for the first second and wondering where she was and why Connel was with her. As her memory came back she scowled at him. 'W...what do you think you're you d...doing?'

'I'm going to undress you and put you to bed,' he coolly informed her, unbuttoning her jade jacket. 'And I've done it before, so don't make a fuss. I'm not going to get over-excited so don't you!'

She pushed his hands away. 'I c...can...'

'No, you can't. You're barely conscious. Just go limp and pretend it isn't happening, and it will be over in a minute.' He unzipped her pants and began pulling them down. 'I'm afraid this suit may never be the same again even when it has been cleaned—it's flecked with mud and broken glass and specks of your blood.'

She shuddered, peering down at the pants. He was right; they were a mess. 'This suit cost a fortune!'

'Never mind, at least you're alive. Now, where will I find clean pyjamas?' he asked, gently lifting her with one arm behind her back to remove her jacket.

'Never mind pyjamas,' she hurriedly said, danger-ously aware of his powerful body close to her, feeling his chest lifting and falling as he breathed, inhaling the scent of him, musky, male, memorable. 'I'll sleep like this.' Something was bothering her. 'How did you get the front door open? And this time don't try and tell me I left it open because I know I locked it!'

'I found the key in your handbag, of course,' he ca-sually said, then laid her down as carefully as if she was made of china, and drew the sheet over her, then the thick, comforting duvet.

'You...you...' she spluttered.

'Yes?' he asked, smiling.

'You had no right to go through my handbag!'

'What was I supposed to do? Sit out there in my car with you all night? Don't be a stupid woman. Try to use the brains God gave you. Now, is there anything I can get you? Milk? Water? A cup of hot chocolate or some tea?'

'No, thank you,' she said through tight lips. His excuse was unanswerable, but then it always was! The man was too clever—how did you cope with a man with a mind like his? She found it hard to believe he was Hal Thaxford's cousin—they were miles apart.

The light went out and she lay in the dark, thinking about him drowsily. She had never met a man like him. He constantly surprised.

With a start she heard him tiptoing across the room and tensed, her pulses jangling.

'What are you doing?' she demanded, ready to fight if he tried to get into bed with her.

'Sorry, did I wake you? I was trying not to make a sound. I suddenly realised you might need a drink of water in the middle of the night so I brought up a jug of water and a glass.' He audibly put them down, the glass clinking against the jug. 'There you are. Anything else you want?'

'No,' she said, still tense. Was that a straightforward question or some sort of proposition?

'Okay. I rang your sister, and she's coming over first thing in the morning.'

'You shouldn't have! Sancha has enough to do already, and she'll bring Flora with her to drive me crazy.'

'She insisted. She would have come tonight, but I told her there was no need to as I would stay with you. You must have somebody here, looking after you, until the risk of concussion is over, and I have to go to work.'

'Did I ask you to stay? I don't need anybody. I can take care of myself.'

'Not in the state you're in! Now, shut up. Go to sleep—if you need me, I'll be in the next room. I found this brass bell in your sitting room—ring that.' She heard it softly chime as he put it down on her already over-crowded bedside table.

He was gone before she could protest and she felt too odd to move. For a few moments she lay there, brooding over his high-handed, infuriating behaviour, but she was too exhausted to stay awake for long. Five minutes later she was fast asleep, and when she woke again it was to find the bedroom full of morning sunshine and a smell of coffee which made her nose twitch. Coffee! Wonderful. That was what she needed.

Gingerly she sat up. Movement still made her wince, but her head wasn't going round and there was nothing wrong with her vision; she could see Connel Hillier perfectly clearly as he walked into the room. Her nerves jumped—freshly shaved, in what was obviously a clean shirt and jeans. How had he managed that? Had he got a travelling wardrobe in his car? And why was he so tall? Every time she saw him he seemed to be taller.

He stopped in his tracks, staring at her, face surprised. 'Oh, you're awake! Why didn't you give me a shout? I would have brought your breakfast up earlier.'

'I only just woke up.'

He was carrying a tray, which he put down across her knees. 'Here you are—orange juice, coffee, boiled eggs and toast. Or do you prefer cereal?'

'No, that looks wonderful,' she said huskily, watching him pull back the curtains to let a sunlit autumn morning into her room. He turned to skate a glance over her and she suddenly realised she was only wearing her bra and panties, and hurriedly pulled the bedclothes up to her neck.

He laughed, giving her that wicked look she remembered from the first time they met, his lashes sweeping his smooth, tanned cheeks. Mockingly he asked, 'Now, what prompted that? Come off it, Zoe—are you trying to convince me you're shy? You of all people?'

Head averted, face cold, she looked at the tray, inhaling the rich odour of the coffee, and said stiffly, 'It's very kind of you to bring me breakfast in bed. I'm not used to it.'

His brows shot up. 'Nobody ever brings you breakfast in bed? No wonder your relationships never last—you date the wrong guys.'

She ignored that, fighting to keep her temper. 'I hope you slept well?'

'Fine,' he said, sounding as if she made him laugh, which didn't improve her mood. 'Did you?'

'Yes, very well, thank you,' she said with icy politeness.

'How do you feel this morning?'

'Stiff as a board, and my ribs hurt.' She spread out her hands for him to see. 'So do my cuts and bruises. But my head's fine now and I haven't any worrying symptoms. No headache, and no eyesight problems.'

'That's good. You look better.' He observed her veiled shape in the bed, eyes dancing. 'What I can see of you.'

Her temper suddenly snapped the rein she had been keeping it on. 'I know you think you're funny, but I'm not in a mood to play games!' she said furiously. 'I don't feel well enough. So will you stop making jokes about the fact that I'm only wearing underclothes and go away?'

He was all innocence, eyes opening wide, face bewildered. 'Did I mention the subject? I never said a word! You're the one obsessed with what you're wearing, not me.'

She felt herself go red. 'You were the one who stared!'

'Sorry,' he said softly. 'Did I? Well, I'm a red-blooded male, not a monk, and when I see a half-naked girl as sexy and beautiful as you are, I can't help staring.'

'Well, try in future!' she muttered, but at the same time registered the compliment. So he thought she was beautiful? And sexy. Heat crept up her body.

He turned away, and she couldn't stop herself staring at him, riveted by the physical impact of that powerful body. He was certainly sexy, not to say beautiful, in his very male way—those wide shoulders and that deep chest, the lean, firm hips and long, long, muscled legs. His very presence in her bedroom when she was half-naked in bed was making her breathless. She had never felt quite so overpowered and aware of a man in her life. It was disturbing to feel like this. Why did he have this effect on her when she didn't even like him?

Or did she? He had charm; she couldn't dispute that. He was kind and thoughtful. He was house-trained and capable, could take care of himself and anyone else who needed it.

She approved of all that—what woman wouldn't? But

he still made her hackles rise, made her bristle with resistance and resentment, because, beneath the apparent 'new man' surface lurked an unregenerate male of the old school, bossy, opinionated, domineering.

He was watching her with narrowed eyes, making her afraid he might be able to read her mind. She would put nothing past him.

'Well, I'll leave you to eat your breakfast and sulk,' he said dryly. 'You have to stay in bed today, whether you feel okay or not. And don't forget to take your pills after breakfast. Your sister should be arriving around ten; she had to get her children dressed and fed first. If you want anything else, ring your bell, remember.'

He went out, and as soon as she heard him going down the stairs she pushed the tray to the end of the bed and carefully slid her legs out. She urgently needed to go to the bathroom before she started on her breakfast.

She went to the lavatory, washed her hands and face rapidly, cleaned her teeth, brushed her tousled hair and put on a short cotton robe over her undies before going back to eat her breakfast. After she had finished she put the tray on the floor and lay back against her pillows to contemplate the morning sky. It was going to be a wonderful day: clear skies, sunshine. Perfect for filming. There had been so much rain lately that they needed a really good day so that they could catch up with the schedule, she thought idly, and then gave a cry of horror.

Filming! She sat up with a jerk. Work! She had forgotten all about it, and the team would be hanging around waiting for her for the second time in a week! They must think she was losing it. She hurriedly got out of bed and looked around for her bag—her mobile would be in it; she must ring immediately to tell them what had happened, and then…

Then what? She couldn't afford to lose any more time—the schedule was shot to hell as it was, and that was disastrous to the budget. She had to work today. Even if she felt like hell.

Whirling, she began taking clothes out of her wardrobe—workman-like jeans, a sweatshirt, a warm wool jacket in a flattering shade of aubergine which complemented her hair.

'What do you think you're doing?' Connel asked sharply from the doorway, before striding across the room and grabbing the clothes from her. He tossed them on to a chair. 'You aren't getting dressed; you're going back to bed.'

'I have to go to work! I should have been there two hours ago. The team will all be waiting; we start at first light. I'm surprised they haven't rung to find out what's happened to me.'

'They have, an hour ago. I explained you had had an accident and would be off work for a few days. Now get back into bed.' He took hold of her arm.

'You did what?' Aghast and angry, she stared at him, tugging free of his restraining hand so violently it sent a stab of pain into her ribs and she had to bite down on her inner lip to stop herself groaning.

Hoarsely, she yelled at him, 'You had no business to tell them any such thing! How dare you interfere like that? I can't afford to miss a day's filming; the company might replace me, permanently, with another director.'

'Not just for the sake of a day or two! You're being paranoid. They'll wait for you to come back if they know it will only be a short delay. You can't go to work, Zoe, it could be dangerous. You may have concussion, you're certainly in pain a lot of the time, and you're obviously still in shock. Get it into your head, woman— you must rest. The doctor knows what he's doing, and he said you mustn't do anything for a few days. That was a very nasty accident you had; you're lucky to be alive.'

'You don't understand film companies—I'm not paranoid; I just know them. The insurance people will demand a new director. It drives them crazy if they think you're going to fall behind with the schedule; even one day's loss means losing money. They're probably already looking for someone to take over from me so that they don't lose any more time.' She turned to pick up her clothes from the chair, where he had flung them, but Connel moved even faster.

He picked her up bodily and carried her, struggling, to her bed, slid her into it and sat down on the edge, leaning over to hold her down by both shoulders.

'It won't do any good to fight me. For once, Zoe, you'll do as you're told!'

A gasp from the open door made them both turn to stare across the room.

Her sister stood there, staring bolt-eyed at them. 'What on earth is going on? Zoe? Are you okay?'

'No, I'm not,' Zoe shouted, flushed and trembling, her green eyes burning with unshed tears of pure rage. 'Get this brute off me. Throw him out of the house.'

Sancha gave Connel an uncertain, worried look. He was her husband's new boss, after all; clearly she wasn't sure how to deal with this situation.

Connel let go of Zoe and stood up, raking back a dishevelled lock of dark hair. 'I found her trying to get dressed to go to work! She must not be allowed to get up, Sancha. She's still in a state of shock and she might have concussion. Make her stay in bed.'

'Get out of my house!' yelled Zoe, half choked at the arrogance and dominating nature of the man.

'I'll get a doctor to deal with her,' he coolly told her sister, without even looking at Zoe.

'You won't do anything of the kind! Go away and don't come back. I never want to set eyes on you again!'

Infuriatingly, he laughed. 'Don't kid yourself.' Turning, he kissed her hard, briefly, on the mouth, making her lips burn, sending a shiver down her spine. 'See you later. Sancha, don't let her get dressed or leave. Make her stay in bed.'

Then he was gone and Sancha stood there staring at her, eyes like saucers and mouth parted.

'What is going on between you two?'

Face hot, body restless in the bed, Zoe wildly said, 'Nothing. Nothing at all. I can't stand the man!'

'Are you sure?' Sancha went on watching her doubtfully.

Angrily, Zoe snapped, 'What do you mean, am I sure? He's everything I hate in a man.'

'If anyone had asked me if he was your type, I'd have said absolutely not,' Sancha agreed. 'But…why did he kiss you? I didn't get the impression it was the first time, either. So, what's going on, Zoe?'

CHAPTER FIVE

THE morning wore on; Zoe lay in bed, half-drowsing, half-worrying about losing another day's filming. She heard her sister hurrying about busily downstairs, putting on the washing machine, vacuuming. At eleven Sancha brought a tray of coffee and biscuits upstairs. Giving her sister a mug of milky coffee and a shortbread biscuit she must have made, because Zoe didn't keep tempting foods in the house, she perched on the side of the bed and smiled. 'The house is spotless, don't worry.'

She got a dry look in response. 'I wasn't! The state of the house was the last thing on my mind. I'm far more anxious about my film. Sancha, listen, you don't want me to be out of work, do you? If I don't turn up again I'll lose my job, surely you can see that?'

'Oh, for goodness' sake—have you forgotten that you nearly killed yourself yesterday? Connel told me your car was a total write-off.'

'But I'm not! I just have a few scratches...'

'You can't see yourself; you look terrible! Horrible blue bruises on your arms and face, not to mention the cuts! And shock takes days to wear off!'

'Oh, thanks, you're such a comfort!'

'I'm not allowing you to leave that bed. Don't think you'll get round me, so drink your coffee and eat your biscuit.'

'I never eat biscuits; they make you fat.' Zoe sipped

her coffee sulkily. 'And I prefer my coffee black! All this milk in it just builds up the calories.'

'I'm building up your immune system—and eat that biscuit; you need the blood sugar! I made them myself, just for you. They're full of energy-giving ingredients.'

'Full of fat and sugar, you mean.' Gloomily surveying the biscuit, Zoe knew she was going to have to eat it to please her sister or Sancha would put on that hurt look she did so well.

'Mark says men prefer women to be cuddly, anyway,' Sancha said, with what Zoe felt was smug complacency.

'Sancha, men prefer their own women to be cuddly and a little plump because they don't want any other man taking a second look! If they could they'd put their wives into a harem, no doubt. But I don't diet to attract men. I diet to stay fit and active and have lots of energy. My job depends on it.'

'Your job depends on your brains, which you aren't using at the moment! Eat your nice biscuit!'

Did Sancha think she was three? No wonder Flora threw things when her mother always talked to her in that tone of voice.

'Sancha, listen...'

'Not until you've eaten your biscuit!'

'Tyrant.' Sighing, Zoe took a bite. Crisp and light and quite delicious; she finished it in three bites. 'You're a great cook,' she told Sancha, who smiled in satisfaction. 'But take the rest of them home to the kids. Don't expect me to eat another single biscuit.'

'All right, but only if you tell me about you and Connel!'

'I already said—nothing to tell!' Zoe finished her coffee. 'You tell me something—how does Mark get on with him? And the truth, now!'

'Mark likes him. He says he's a great guy, straight-forward, easy to talk to, prepared to listen if a problem comes up. The men like Connel too, even though he's not a push-over when it comes to one of them making trouble.' Sancha's eyes were bright and watchful, gleam-ing with curiosity. 'And he left this place like a new pin. He'd not only washed up after breakfast, he had tidied the kitchen, and made the bed he's using.'

Zoe's heart distinctly tumbled inside her chest, like a fish leaping up in water. Why had her sister used the present tense? Connel had gone. Hadn't he?

'What do you mean—using? Used, you mean, just for last night. He's not one of the fixtures and fittings.'

Sancha gazed at her intently, a little smile curling her mouth. 'But he's coming back tonight.'

'No, he is not!' Agitated, Zoe sat up against her pil-lows. 'What made you think he was?'

'Why, he did!' Sancha became serious. 'Zoe, I can't stay on here all night. I have to get back to take care of the boys and Mark, but you must have someone here, just in case a problem comes up during the night. After a crash like that all sorts of reaction can set in without warning. Shock can be very dangerous. So when Connel said he would do the night shift I was grateful. I didn't think you'd object.'

'You didn't ask!'

'Well, he took care of you last night, and you seemed happy enough about that. So I assumed it was okay to accept his offer.'

Zoe ground her teeth together to stop herself bursting

out with the fury she felt. She knew that would worry Sancha.

Her sister was already worried, watching her uneasily. 'You know I'd love to have you stay with us, but we don't have a spare bedroom. Unless...' She frowned in thought, chewing her lower lip. 'Well, the boys could move back in together again, and then you could have the little spare room, but I'm afraid it's full of Charlie's toys and...oh, it wouldn't take me long to clear the room, I expect.'

Zoe heard the note of panic in her sister's voice; a picture of Charlie's tiny box room flashed into her mind—model planes on strings hanging from the ceiling, posters of cars and *Star Wars* on the walls, toys on every available surface. It would take Sancha an age to make it habitable for an adult, and it only held a narrow, cramped little bed.

'No, no, don't even think about it,' she quickly said. 'I would prefer to be in my own home. Even if it means putting up with Connel Hillier for a while.' She faked a wide yawn. 'I'm sleepy again. I can't understand it. I've slept for hours already.'

'It's the shock. And those pills.' Sancha carried the coffee tray towards the door. 'I'll have to pop out to check on the kids. Martha's looking after them but she'll need a break from Flora soon.'

'I bet!'

Her sister looked reproachfully at her. 'Look, you just have a sleep and I'll bring you your lunch when I get back.'

Zoe lay back and shut her eyes. Ten minutes dragged past before she heard her sister driving away. Jumping out of bed, Zoe picked up the phone, rang for a taxi, then got dressed hurriedly. Sancha would be furious with her, but her job mattered too much to risk losing it. Sancha had no idea how vital money was in the film business, how much you could lose by losing a day or two, and how ruthless the film business could be if you threatened the prompt wrapping up of a film.

A quarter of an hour later, in blue jeans and a warm, camel-coloured sweatshirt, she was on her way to a local garage where she had often hired a car in the past. The manager had already heard about her crash, and observed her even more closely than he usually did. He was never offensive with his interest in her, simply one of those men who always register the way a woman looks.

'I was expecting you to look terrible, but apart from a few cuts I'd hardly know you had had an accident. I hear the same couldn't be said about your car! A total write-off, isn't it? You'll be needing a new one—come and see what I've got,' he invited, but she shook her head.

'No time today—I'll pop in on Saturday.'

'Now, don't you go elsewhere, Zoe. I'll give you a good deal,' he assured her as she drove off in his blue Ford hire car.

They were filming on location an hour's drive from her home. They had broken for lunch when she drove up. Most of the actors were sitting in their caravans, eating the salad meal the caterers had provided. Some of the crew were eating that too, but others were eating sausages and chips swimming in baked beans. They all turned their heads to stare as she got out of the car. A ripple of murmured comment broke out.

Will, in grubby jeans sagging at the hips and a mud-smeared sweatshirt, came to meet her, grinning as his eyes slid quickly over the visible evidence of her crash.

'You fraud! There's nothing wrong with you—and I just sent you flowers!' He folded her in his arms and hugged her; it was like being embraced by a shambling bear smelling of machine oil.

'That was nice of you, Will,' she said, gently detaching herself without making it obvious. 'Who's directing?'

Will grimaced his rugged face wry. 'The company's looking for someone, but at the moment I'm carrying on with your schedule, using the shooting script and your notes. I asked them if I could and they agreed, in the hope that you'd be back in a day or so. I shot Scene 45 this morning, no dialogue, just a slow pan of the landscape, and I've blocked out that short snatch of dialogue between Fran and Philip. We went over it while they were having lunch in their caravans. The light's fine, and I didn't think they'd need much direction, they're both so good.' He eyed her uncertainly, not sure how she would react, and she smiled reassurance at him.

'Great. I don't know why I bothered to come; obviously you can manage without me.'

'Rubbish,' he said, instantly. 'You'd talked me through today's schedule on Friday. I knew what you wanted me to do, and so did the actors. We just carried on with your instructions. You always prepare so well, as I said to Ben Green.'

'And what did he say?' she dryly asked. The managing director of the company backing the film, a bald, eagle-eyed man in his fifties, was usually fair-minded, but when money was at stake he could be difficult. An accountant and a lawyer, he was good at his job but obsessed with the cost of everything, always looking to cut corners financially.

'He said he knew you did, and we were to go ahead with what you had laid down for today while he thought about who to replace you with if you didn't come back soon.'

'You probably saved my job!' Zoe sighed. 'Thanks, Will. I'll just get myself some salad, and then we'll start work again. If you don't mind, I would like to check how you blocked the scene before we shoot. I'm sure you did a great job, but I need to know how it looks.'

'Sure, of course,' he said. 'I'll get the stand-ins out to take up the positions. Do you want to check the scene I shot? I can get it up on video for you?'

'Oh, I'm sure you did your usual brilliant job, Will. I'll see it this evening when we look through everything we shot today.'

As Zoe walked over to the caterers' caravan her production runner, Barbara, hurried over to join her, a slim girl in workman-like dark blue dungarees and a bright yellow shirt.

'I thought you weren't coming to work today? The guy who answered your phone this morning said you would be off sick for several days.' Barbara's bright hazel eyes were taking in her cuts and bruises. 'From what he told me about this crash, you were lucky to get off with just a few minor injuries.'

'Very lucky,' agreed Zoe emphatically, turning to order salad from the girl behind the counter.

Chewing gum and looking bored, the girl asked, 'Tuna and peach or cheese?'

'Tuna, please.' Zoe looked with disfavour at the girl's rather grubby-looking scarlet talons as they unwrapped Clingfilm from a salad taken out of the small fridge at the back.

'Drink?' the girl yawned.

'Just mineral water, thanks.'

Going back to the fridge, the girl took out a bottle, turned to clatter it down on Zoe's tray. 'Pudding? We've got fruit or cake.'

'No pudding, thanks. By the way, your hands need washing, have you noticed? Will you do that now?'

She got a poisonous look, but as she walked away the girl went to the sink and began noisily washing her hands, muttering, 'Who does she think she is? Bitch. My hands are perfectly clean.'

Barbara giggled. 'She's not going to love you.'

'Do I care? It would cost us a fortune if she spread salmonella among the cast and crew.'

Barbara kept pace with her and after a pause asked, 'He sounded tough—who was he?'

Without looking at her, Zoe frowned. 'Who was who?'

'The guy I talked to on the phone this morning. It wasn't your brother-in-law, was it?'

'No, it wasn't Mark,' Zoe said curtly.

Barbara's bright, curious eyes watched her eagerly. 'Someone new? Is he good-looking? He sounds it.'

'How can you sound good-looking, for heaven's sake?'

'He has a sexy voice!'

Zoe felt as if she had been punched in the stomach. Her lungs fought for breath. It was only too true—Connel had a deep, velvety, gorgeous voice, as sexy as hell.

'I hadn't noticed,' she huskily lied, sitting down at the small table in her caravan and beginning to eat. Barbara stood at the door, watching her. 'Were there any messages for me?' Zoe asked her curtly.

'Only one from Casting—Lee Williams won't be playing the policeman. He's gone into hospital with appendicitis. They've replaced him with Hal Thaxford.'

Zoe turned appalled eyes on her. 'You're kidding!'

Barbara grinned with a gleeful triumph. 'I knew you wouldn't like it.'

Grinding her teeth, Zoe muttered, 'Like it? Understatement of the year. Jenny knows I hate working with Pinocchio. What does she think she's doing? Surely they could have found somebody better than him!'

'Apparently, nobody was free at the time. She said she'd tried, but had no luck. Do you want me to get her on the line for you?'

'I haven't got time now; I'll ring her later.' Zoe concentrated on her food. 'Tell them I'll be on the set in five minutes, will you, Bar?'

Barbara hurried away. As she drank her cold, sparkling water Zoe stared at nothing. Connel Hillier was problem enough. She did not need Hal Thaxford around too, especially after hearing from Connel what Hal had said about her. Heartless, manipulative, cruel... Her teeth met. And Connel had believed every word!

Well, at least she would get a chance to tell Hal Thaxford precisely what she thought of him, and she wouldn't spare her language, either.

Maybe he would think twice about spreading vicious gossip about her if she threatened to sue him!

Loading her tray again, she got up and carried it out of the caravan, handed it to Barbara to take back to Catering, and started work.

The sun was sinking by the time she finished shooting the scene. 'Tomorrow we'll shoot Scene 70; it's another short one, with Fran and Dexter this time. Only a page of dialogue; we don't need a rehearsal. Wrap it up for me, would you, Will?' she asked, conscious of weariness. Her head was aching badly, her body was stiff, her ribs hurt every time she took a breath.

'Sure. Are you okay? You're very pale.' He stared at her in concern and she managed a tired smile.

'I'll be fine once I get home. See you tomorrow, Will.'

The drive home was an ordeal; she was dying to get home, have a hot bath, get to bed. It took all her energy to keep her mind on driving. She couldn't even think, just drove on automatic pilot. She didn't want another crash!

As she finally turned in through her own gates she looked uneasily towards the cottage, afraid to see lights on inside, which would mean that Sancha was waiting for her, full of reproaches and recrimination. Zoe was too tired to face her sister tonight, so she was deeply relieved to see that the house was dark; there was nobody there.

With accustomed skill rather than decision, she parked outside in her usual spot, got out, yawning and shivering.

The day's work had been rather more of a strain than she had anticipated. She would be filming again tomorrow, yet in her heart she knew she would much rather stay at home, in bed. Not that she would have admitted that, especially to Sancha. Or Connel. No, never to him. Her job meant more than anything else in her life; she had to be there on the set, tomorrow, even if she felt like death warmed up.

There were no other houses in view, no street lights, and the stars were veiled in cloud, making the darkness seem impenetrable as she walked to the front door. Her nerves prickled at something in the atmosphere—a faint sighing, which was probably only the wind in the trees, an expectation which had to be her own imagination. There was nobody there, yet she felt as if someone was watching her, someone was waiting in the shadows, making a shiver run down her spine.

She had her key out before she reached the door, it turned in the lock and she took a step inside the cottage, but at that second something moved behind her, there was a noise on the gravel, like hurrying feet, then somebody cannoned into her, hit from the back and propelled her forward, the force of that impact sending her toppling helplessly, full length on the carpet.

Winded, she lay there for a second, gasping for breath. Connel had gone too far this time! How dared he knock her over like that? She began to struggle up, but a second later hands grabbed her, pulled her up, turned her face upwards.

'What do you think you're doing…?' she angrily began, only to be silenced by a mouth coming down on her open lips.

Suffocating, Zoe fought to push him away. His hands were touching her in a way that scared her stiff, pushing up under her jacket, under her sweatshirt, fondling her breasts.

This wasn't Connel. She knew the smell of Connel, his build, his firm, cool hands. This wasn't him.

Who was it? In God's name, who was it? And what...what did he plan to do to her?

Fear paralysed her; she trembled, cold sweat on her skin, her throat thick with dread.

CHAPTER SIX

FROM the garden a cold wind blew in through the open door, chilling her even more, but in a different way, kick-starting her brain again. She had once filmed a women's self-defence course—they had dealt with just such a situation as this. What had the tutor advised them to do?

Deliberately she removed her mind from the panic and terror of what he was doing to her body. She didn't always remember what was said, but she rarely forgot anything she saw. Her mind flashed her an image of a hall full of women. Yes, that was it!

Pulling her head as far back as she could, she went for his eyes, pushing her thumbs into both at the same time, while in the same instant she pulled a knee up as hard as she could into his groin.

He gave a grunt of pain and let go of her breasts, his hands reaching up to push her thumbs out of his eyes.

'You bitch, that hurt!'

'Get off me!' she yelled, her hands now screwed into fists, and began hitting him in the face. She kicked him, too, in the shins, on the ankles, with a force that made one of her shoes fly off.

He was swearing viciously, trying to hold her down, control her again, and suddenly Zoe recognised his voice.

'Larry!'

He stopped swearing, lay still for a few seconds, then gave a hoarse, strangled groan.

'You...you bastard!' she breathed hoarsely. 'Get off me!' She had never been afraid of Larry, only disturbed by that obsessive nature of his. Angrily she shoved him away.

'Zoe...listen...I wouldn't have hurt you...I just wanted to...needed to...hold you, touch you. I love you. You know I do.'

'If this is your idea of love, God help you,' she bit out. 'Now, will you get up?'

Silently, he scrambled off her and stood up. Zoe got up too, and reached for the light switch, blinking as the darkness was flooded with bright light.

Larry winced from the illumination, head held down, not meeting her eyes. There were swelling bruises on his face, a smear of blood from his nose.

Zoe stared at him. 'How could you do a thing like this? What did you intend to do to me? Rape me? Kill me?'

Just saying it made her blood run cold. Until her mind started working he had been winning; she had been so scared she might not have stopped him, out of sheer terror. Now she knew just how a woman felt when a man jumped her out of the dark. Fear was the enemy as much as any rapist.

'No,' Larry muttered. 'No, I wouldn't have... Zoe, I love you. I wouldn't have hurt you.'

Her cat-like green eyes spat rage and contempt. 'Love me? Oh, that's why you knocked me to the floor and tried to scare the living daylights out of me? You have a funny idea of love!'

'I kept ringing; you wouldn't talk to me! You wouldn't see me. I was desperate.'

'So you attacked me! Did you really think you could get away with it? After all those threatening phone calls the police would have been on to you in two seconds flat; you would have been the obvious suspect, and no matter how much you lied a simple DNA test would soon have proved it was you! You might have gone to prison for years.'

'You made me love you and then you dumped me!' he said in that familiar, petulant, childish voice, and she looked at him with contempt.

'I didn't make you do anything of the kind! Nobody can make anybody love them, and if you cared twopence for me you wouldn't be here now; you wouldn't feel justified in hurting me!'

'You hurt me!'

'I may have damaged your ego; I don't believe I hurt you. It's not me you're obsessed with; it's yourself.'

He looked as if she'd hit him again. 'How can you be so cruel? If I did attack you, you deserved it. You know I love you, but you treat me like a stray dog.' He was dark red now and breathing thickly. Suddenly he went for her again, his hands reaching for her throat, taking her off guard again.

Choking, her ears buzzing, Zoe tried to fight free, but Larry was in a frenzied state. His hands were stronger than she had realised; she couldn't pull them down from her throat. Her eyes clouded, she felt herself losing consciousness, and then abruptly he let go of her. Zoe reeled back and fell against the wall, coughing and retching, breathing painfully.

Her eyes were still clouded, but dimly she saw some-one who hadn't been there before. Another man. He must have pulled Larry off her. Who was it? she thought stupidly. And where on earth had he come from just in the nick of time?

She looked through the open front door. A car was parked outside. The cold night air was clearing her brain. She knew that car. Shakily, she pushed hair back from her eyes and looked at the newcomer again.

'Are you okay?' Connel's deep voice asked, and she laughed wildly at the question.

Hoarsely, she whispered, 'I'll live!'

'You're lucky I got here in time! I'll ring the police.'

'Wait...' she said, touching his arm, and he halted, looking down at her with a frown.

'Where's Larry? Has he gone?' she asked, and the dark eyes narrowed, hard as obsidian.

'You know him?'

She nodded, and his mouth tightened.

After a pause, he glanced sideways and her gaze fol-lowed his. Larry lay on the floor at the foot of the stairs, on his back. His eyes were shut but his mouth was open.

'What's the matter with him?'

'I knocked him out,' Connel curtly told her.

'He looks dead!'

'He isn't.'

She was worried. 'Are you sure?'

'If you'd stop talking for a second you'd hear him breathing.'

She didn't like the aggressive tone, or the way he was looking at her. In the silence between them she heard

Larry breathing like a boiling kettle through his open mouth, and looked at him with uneasy concern.

'He sounds odd—how hard did you hit him?'

Scowling, Connel said, 'When I got here I found him trying to kill you—and when I dragged him away from you he turned on me so I punched him in the face. I simply hit him hard enough to make sure he cooled down. Now, if you've finished your inquisition, I'll go and ring the police.' He turned to walk towards the sitting room and she shouted after him.

'No!'

In mid-step he stopped and looked back at her, black brows lifting incredulously.

'What do you mean—no? He was trying to strangle you. The man's dangerous. If you don't call the police he'll try again, and you may not be so lucky next time. If I hadn't turned up when I did you could be dead by now.'

His raised voice had penetrated the fog in Larry's brain; he stirred, groaned, began to struggle into a sitting position, holding his jaw.

'W...w...what happened?' Blearily, he looked around and saw them; Zoe watched awareness flash into his eyes. 'Oh...' he moaned, as his gaze moved on to take in Connel's frowning face. Taking a deep breath, Larry grunted, 'Was it him who hit me?'

'Yes, and I'll do it again if you make the wrong move,' threatened Connel in a voice that meant every word he said.

Larry gingerly rubbed his jawline. 'It feels as if I've been hit by a truck. I'm going to sue you, mister! You could have killed me, hitting me that hard!'

'You can tell the police when they get here,' snapped Connel.

Alarm came into Larry's eyes. 'Police?' He staggered to his feet. 'You...you've rung the police?' He looked reproachfully at Zoe. 'You didn't? How could you when you know I'd never have hurt you. I love you; you know I do. Haven't you done enough to me? Making me love you, then dumping me, refusing to see me, or even talk to me? You drive me insane, and then you call the police—you're determined to ruin my life, aren't you? You won't be satisfied until I'm in prison, out of a job, my whole life destroyed!'

Wearily, Zoe said, 'Oh, go away, Larry. He hasn't rung the police. But if you ever come near me again, I will. No more phone calls or letters! And never, ever, come to my home again unless you want to end up in a cell.'

'Zoe...don't be so heartless!' he groaned, coming towards her with his hands held out. 'I'm sorry...forgive me...I love you...'

She looked at him scornfully. 'No, you don't, or you wouldn't have tried to strangle me. If you love someone, you don't want to hurt them. You love yourself, Larry. Not me.'

'I can't stop thinking about you; I can't sleep—just give me one more chance, Zoe! It isn't much to ask, is it?'

Connel harshly ground out through his teeth, 'That's enough of that, sunshine. You heard her. She doesn't want you here. On your way and don't come back, or you'll have me to deal with.'

Larry looked wildly at him, then at Zoe. 'Is he why

you dumped me? I suspected it was something like that. There had to be another man—with you, there's always another man, isn't there?'

Furious, she opened her mouth to deny it, but he didn't give her the chance. Looking at Connel with bitterness, he sneered, 'You'll find out what she's like! It will be your turn next for the treatment. Don't let yourself care too much—she waits until you're crazy about her and then she dumps you. She's as cold as ice and as cruel as a cat playing with a half-dead mouse.'

Zoe flinched at the accusation. It wasn't true. Of course it wasn't. She wasn't cold. Or cruel.

Connel's dark eyes flicked to her face, then back to Larry. Brusquely, he muttered, 'You've had your say. Come on, you're leaving.' Grabbing Larry's collar, he frogmarched him out of the cottage before slamming the front door on him.

Zoe unsteadily walked into the kitchen, put on the light, then sat down before her legs gave way. She didn't want to humiliate herself in front of Connel by fainting, but she was chilled to the bone and shivering. Of course, she was tired after working for hours in the open air, and on top of that being attacked by Larry when she got back here.

Connel followed her into the room, gave her a hard, searching look, then without a word began to make tea.

Over his shoulder as he set out mugs he said icily, 'You know, I was beginning to think Hal had been wrong about you, but obviously he had your number spot-on. You've destroyed that stupid guy. I wish now I hadn't hit the poor bastard so hard.'

'Go away,' she yelled at him, fighting with tears and

a sense of injustice. 'Get out of my house. Right now. And don't come back.'

'What's the matter, Zoe? Afraid of the truth?' The biting tone was like a scalpel boring into her heart; she lifted her head, clouds of red hair spilling around her white face, to look at him with pain and anger.

'It isn't the truth! If I go out with someone and realise I don't want it to get serious, what am I supposed to do? Marry him even if he bores me rigid? Haven't you ever dated someone then realised she was the wrong woman for you? If you can, why shouldn't I? Don't I have the right to change my mind?'

His eyes watched her, hard as black glass, glittering.

It made her even edgier to have him look at her that way. She bit her lip, but ploughed on huskily. 'Larry, for instance— I liked him when I met him, but then he started telling me endlessly about his previous girl-friends. He wanted me to be jealous. If we bumped into some girl he had once dated he was ecstatic, and kept telling me I didn't need to be jealous, but it was obvious he hoped I would be and he got sulky when I wasn't.'

His mouth twisted. 'I suppose he was right in a way— jealousy would have meant you cared.'

She had to admit that. 'I suppose so—but I wasn't in love with him, so I had to stop seeing him. You must see that? All his attempts to make me jealous got on my nerves. Even worse, he wanted me to tell him all about the guys I'd been out with—but I wouldn't do that, either. I don't believe in talking about one man to another; once a relationship is over it's over, and it isn't fair to them to talk about them behind their back.'

'No,' he agreed, frowning. 'Most men would hate that. Including me.'

She laughed roughly. 'That I can imagine.' Oh, yes, she knew that much about him. He was a man with strong ideas about himself; he would hate to know a woman was spreading gossip about him. She viewed him with some sympathy. That was one thing they had in common.

'I wouldn't want a guy talking about me to other women,' she said. 'But Larry was determined to know who else I'd been out with and whether I'd slept with them. I refused to tell him anything, but he kept on and on about it—he's the obsessive type, only it's himself he's really obsessed with. He sees everyone else in relation to himself and never sees any other point of view. I explained that I don't believe in talking about what's over, but he simply refused to accept that. He wouldn't accept that I didn't want to see him again, either. He's been ringing and writing ever since! He wouldn't give up. But I didn't think he was crazy enough to show up and actually attack me!'

Connel put a cup of tea in front of her. 'Just as well I turned up when I did. God knows what would have happened if I hadn't. Have you eaten?'

She stared blankly, not remembering for a second, and he angrily muttered at her, 'You haven't, have you? You make me so furious! Are you trying to make yourself really ill? When your sister rang me and told me you had got dressed and gone off while she was collecting her little girl I wanted to follow you and make you come back, but I didn't know where the film was being made and your sister had no idea either, nor did she have a phone number for the film company.'

'Well, I'm glad about that!' she muttered, glaring. 'I wouldn't have appreciated being arrested and dragged away from my job in front of the whole film crew! Who do you think you are?'

'You shouldn't have gone back to work immediately after that accident.'

'I didn't want my film being handed over to someone else! You don't understand...'

He bent down close to her, his dark eyes boring into hers. 'No, it's you who doesn't understand! Shock can kill! This might be your last film if you don't listen to reason!'

'I'm fine,' she said obstinately, shifting away from the menace of that strong face. Her heart hurt against her ribs at being so close to him. 'Stop invading my body space!'

His eyes gleamed in a new way. 'Am I, Zoe?' he whispered, and her throat fluttered with awareness.

'Stop threatening me! First Larry, then you! What's wrong with men lately? Why are they so aggressive? Why do they think they know what's best for other people? Why do they try to push people around?'

'I don't know about Larry, but as to me—I'm only trying to make you listen to reason!' He put out a hand to brush her tousled red hair back from her face; his long fingers light and gentle. 'You're such a fool, Zoe. Your own worst enemy.'

Oh, God, that was true! she thought, swallowing hard. She was a fool. The sound of his deep voice, the brush of his fingers, had made her feel weak, as if she might faint on the floor at his feet any minute. He was far too close. She averted her eyes from the temptation of that wide, powerful mouth, but could still see every line of it. She couldn't remember ever wanting to be kissed with such a deep ache of need and it appalled her. What on earth was wrong with her? Maybe he was right and she was still in shock, if not actually off her head! It was the only explanation for the crazy way she felt.

'Your skin's cold,' he said, stroking her cheek. 'Drink your tea while I make some food. I haven't eaten, either. What have you got in your fridge?'

'Nothing much,' she said, picking up her cup and holding it gratefully between her shivering hands. The warmth of the tea made her feel better, but she was still very shaky as she sipped the sweet, milky liquid and watched him opening the fridge.

'What do you mean? There's plenty of food in here.'

Over his shoulder she saw he was right. 'Sancha must have done some shopping for me; that was good of her.'

Connel gave her a dry glance. 'Especially after you ran out on her—she's furious with you about that, by the way. She was very upset when she got back here and found you gone.'

She must ring Sancha and apologise, but not tonight. She wasn't up to it. It would have to be tomorrow.

He straightened, inspecting a plate he held in his hand. 'How about steak? There's enough here for two, and it would only take a few minutes to cook. I cook a lot of steak. I see Sancha stocked up on vegetables; there's mushrooms and tomatoes and I could microwave a jacket potato unless you want chips.'

'No, jacket potato would be fine. I rarely eat chips,

too high in calories.' She put down her cup and began to get up. 'I'll help.'

He whirled and put his hands on her shoulders. 'Sit down again. I'm doing the cooking. All I want you to do is sit by the radiator and stay warm.'

'You big bully,' she huskily said, trembling again at how it felt to be so close to his powerful, warm body. She had the most stupid yearning to lean on him, put her arms round him and cling. What was the matter with her? She had never wanted to cling to any man before. She had never been the clinging type—the opposite, in fact!

He walked away, came back with a glass of orange juice. 'Here, drink this while I heat up some soup for you. I remember you said you liked it. There's some fresh soup in the fridge, I see—tomato and basil or asparagus. Which would you like?'

'Tomato, thank you.' She sipped her juice, watching him in a sort of trance as he moved around. He was beginning to look as if he belonged in her kitchen and that was even more worrying. Familiarity was dangerous, so was habit—if she wasn't careful she would start missing him when he wasn't here.

Putting the waxed soup box into the microwave, he quickly flicked the control buttons to switch the oven on, then began dealing with the other ingredients, washing and drying the steak, slicing tomatoes, rubbing oil into the outer skin of the potato before sprinkling it with salt. His deftness and speed were impressive.

A few minutes later Zoe had a bowl of hot soup in front of her. Connel gave her a soup spoon and a roll and butter.

'You get on with that while I finish cooking the meal.'

She bent over to inhale the scent, sighing. 'Smells delicious. Aren't you going to have some?'

'No. I'll just have the steak. It will be ready in ten minutes, so start eating the soup.'

It was like being married, she thought, taking her first spoonful. He gave her his orders as if he had every right to run her life. She ought to do something about that, but just now she felt too cold and tired. Next time she saw him she would tell him where to jump. If she felt normal enough.

'Is it okay?' Connel asked her, and she nodded, taking some more.

'It tastes as good as it smells.'

The rest of the meal was as marvellous; he had cooked the steak to perfection, although he had given her too much. She couldn't eat it all, and by the time she had finished her meal she was heavy-eyed and drowsy.

'No coffee,' Connel told her, studying her across the kitchen table. 'Bed for you now.'

'Not after eating all that food!'

'You're asleep where you sit!' he mocked, and she laughed, knowing he was right. She was barely able to keep her eyes open.

'Well, first I'll help you clear the kitchen and wash up!'

'That won't take me five minutes. Upstairs with you, Zoe—or do you want me to carry you and undress you?'

Heat burned in her face. Her eyes couldn't hold the mockery in his; she looked away. 'I certainly don't!' She got up too fast and hit her knee on the table-leg, staggered slightly, grunting in pain.

Connel's arms went round her. 'Now what have you done?'

Her throat closed in alarm. 'Nothing, I'm okay.' She pushed at his wide shoulders without making any impact on him at all. Indeed, he laughed, looking down into her flushed face, his eyes darkly bright.

Softly he said, 'Why are you in such a panic, Zoe? What are you afraid of? Me? Or yourself?'

'I'm not afraid of you or myself,' she lied, ice trickling down her spine in spite of the curious fact that her body was burning. If anyone had asked a month ago what sort of person she was, she would have said she was a cool, clear-headed professional woman. Someone rational and balanced. Not given to extremes. Now she was suddenly a battleground for violent swings of feeling, of reaction and counter-reaction, back and forth, and it was deeply disturbing.

'Sure about that?' Connel's head bent, his warm mouth brushed her neck, and she took a deep, shaken breath.

'Don't!'

She shifted her head back out of reach, giving his shoulders another shove. He was like a wall, big and immovable, and it made her dizzy to find her head so far back. 'I don't want you kissing me!'

'Don't you, Zoe?' His mouth slid inch by inch upwards from her throat. She knew he was going to kiss her and she told herself to stop him, wrench herself free, escape, but she didn't have the energy or strength.

His mouth finally touched hers and her fingernails dug into his shirt in fierce reaction. Her lips parted; her eyes shut. She kissed him back with a passion she couldn't dam, a desire that rose like floodwaters in her body, taking her away with them.

She couldn't think. A chilliness crept through her, darkness engulfed her. Her knees really gave and she slowly slid down backwards, unable to hold on to consciousness.

The next thing she knew she was apparently whirling through the air. Her lids flickered, lifted; she wildly looked around and realised she was being carried across her shadowy bedroom.

She looked up into the hard, male strength of the face just above her.

'Ah...you've come to,' Connel said huskily close to her ear.

'What happened?'

'You fainted.'

'I never fainted in my life!' she protested.

'Well, there's a first time for everything,' he said, putting her down on her bed and leaning over to switch on her bedside lamp. 'What do you want to wear in bed?'

Alarm bells at once began ringing in her head. 'Never mind. I can manage.' She struggled up against the pillows, defensively watching him. 'Leave the washing up; I'll do it tomorrow. Thank you for being so kind—cooking and...it was a lovely meal. But...but I'd rather you left now.'

He gave her a mocking look. 'Afraid I'm going to climb in bed with you?'

'No! I...no...' she stammered, knowing that was exactly what she was afraid of.

Through his dark lashes his eyes glinted. 'Don't

worry. When I make love to you I'd prefer you to be wide awake and very aware of what I'm doing.'

So would she, but, flushed and trembling like a leaf, she glared at him.

'You won't be making love to me! Now or in the future!'

He smiled and her heart turned over heavily.

'Oh, yes, Zoe. I will.'

'Go away!' she whispered, wanting him to leave before he could see just how vulnerable she was to him.

'Sure you can manage to undress? I'm getting quite good at it. I seem to do it all the time.'

The teasing in his voice made her want to scream.

'Will you go?' she hoarsely demanded.

He turned and walked out, saying over his shoulder, 'If you need me...for anything...I'll be downstairs for the next half-hour or so. Just give me a yell.'

She waited until he had gone downstairs before rushing over to lock her bedroom door, then she undressed, went into the bathroom for a few minutes, and put on pyjamas before climbing back into bed, setting her alarm clock for the usual time. She refused to think about Connel or her own weird, inexplicable reactions to him. Within minutes of her head hitting the pillow she was fast asleep.

Her alarm clock seemed to go off half an hour later. Yawning, she reached to silence it, still half-asleep. She had slept like the dead, and if the alarm hadn't woken her she knew she would have slept on and on for hours. She longed to fall back into bed and sleep again, but she had to get to work, so she struggled out of bed and into the bathroom, took a quick shower and got dressed in jeans and a white T-shirt over which she put a green V-necked sweater.

Zoe strapped on her wristwatch, trod into shoes, unlocked her bedroom door, opened it, and stood there, listening. There wasn't a sound.

Then as she was halfway downstairs her nostrils quivered. Coffee! Bacon!

Moving faster, she ran to the kitchen and stopped dead. Connel was sitting at the kitchen table drinking coffee. He lazily looked her up and down, brows lifting.

'You look very workman-like. If you think you're going to work, you can forget it. The doctor ordered you to rest, and you're staying here, resting, until he gives you the all-clear.'

Outrage filled her. 'Don't you give me orders! I have to go to work. How many times do I have to explain? The company will hand my film over to someone else if I don't show up. Time is money in our business. We can't afford to lose a day. I can't take any more time off. And, anyway, I'm fine. I slept all night. I feel great.'

He studied her. 'You look better, I'll admit that, but I think you're taking a stupid risk. I can't stop you going to work—I have important appointments myself, I can't take the day off, either, and your sister won't get here until ten o'clock. I'll ring her and tell her not to come, but you must at least have some breakfast. Sit down and eat some bacon and egg.'

'I'll just have some fruit and a cup of coffee.' She sat down, though, and watched him pour her coffee, absorbing the fact that he was wearing different clothes this morning: a very elegant dark striped suit, a crisp blue-striped shirt, a sleek dark blue silk tie. Either he had gone home last night, or he had brought a change of clothes with him, which must mean that he had intended to spend the night here. He had shaved; his hair was brushed smoothly. He looked very sexy.

Far too sexy. She looked away, her heart apparently lodged in her throat, making it hard to swallow the coffee she was sipping.

Connel walked across the room and came back with a glass of ice-cold orange juice which he put in front of her.

'Thanks. Don't let me stop you cooking yourself breakfast. I shall have to go in five minutes, anyway,' she said, without looking at him.

He went back to the hob. She heard him cooking, heard toast pop up, then he came over to her with a plate.

'Eat this or you don't leave the house without a fight!'

She stared at the grilled bacon, fried egg and toast on the plate. They smelt wonderful. Hunger stirred in her but she obstinately said, 'I told you, I don't eat breakfast. There isn't time and it's easier to work if you haven't eaten.'

'Make time.' There was an inexorable note in his voice. Zoe gave him a quick, reluctant glance and saw the insistence in his jawline, in his hard mouth, his dark eyes. He meant to make a fight of it, that was obvious, and she simply couldn't afford to waste energy on another long wrangle with him.

Grimly, she picked up the knife and fork he had put on the table, and began to eat.

Sitting down opposite her, Connel ate too. He had the same meal. 'Tell me about your film,' he invited. 'Who's in it?'

She told him a few names. 'And I just heard that your cousin is taking over a part. Someone dropped out.'

'Hal? If I'd known that I'd have rung him yesterday to find out where you were filming.' He gave her an amused look. 'You aren't one of his fans, are you?'

'No.' She had finished her food; she drank the last of her coffee and got up. 'I must rush. I'm going to be late now, anyway. I'll ring Sancha from our location, apologise for yesterday and tell her not to bother to come over today.'

Connel followed her to the front door. 'Put on a warm coat. The weather's turning cold today, according to the forecast on the news this morning.'

She shrugged into a tartan wool-lined anorak, put on driving gloves, wishing he would stop giving her orders. 'Bye.'

'See you later,'' he ominously said as she unlocked her hire car.

He stood in the open front door watching her drive away, waved as she turned out of the drive. Zoe waved back. It was like being married. Saying goodbye to your husband before going to work. She had never actually lived with a man. Her relationships had never been deep enough, long enough.

With a sinking heart, she realised she liked it. She was enjoying having him there all the time, cooking for her, looking after her, being protective, making her put on a warm coat, waving goodbye to her—even if it annoyed her and made her hackles rise.

Oh, God, he's getting under my skin! she thought. He's beginning to be part of my life as no man ever has.

What am I going to do about him?

CHAPTER SEVEN

SHE rang Sancha on her mobile while she was waiting for Will to move camera position after the first short scene they'd shot that morning. Everyone else was busy. The stand-ins were frozen in position where the actual stars would stand when filming started; Andy, their Grip, was setting up a circular track system so that Will could film the next but one scene in the round, and Props were checking that all requirements for this scene had been met. The actors were in their caravans, making sure they knew their lines and positions. Catering were preparing a fried breakfast to be eaten during the next break. The smell of hot fat made Zoe's nose wrinkle.

It took some time for Sancha to answer, but as soon as she heard Zoe's voice, her sister burst out furiously, 'Oh, it's you! You've got a nerve, ringing me after walking out on me yesterday. I was really worried. How could you just disappear without even leaving a note?'

'I'm sorry, but...'

'My imagination worked overtime. I could imagine you passing out as you were driving along a road, crashing again, and being killed this time. I didn't know whether to ring the police or...so I rang Mark to see if his boss had any idea where you had gone, and...'

Flushed, Zoe snapped, 'Yes, he told me—Sancha, you shouldn't have done that! I don't want that man getting the idea that he has any authority over me!'

'What are you talking about? What authority? I simply asked him if he knew where you might have gone.'

Zoe kept her voice down, not wishing the whole crew to hear this argument. 'It must have been obvious where I'd gone. To work. I was afraid I'd lose my film. I had to…'

'They wouldn't sack you just because you were off sick after such a serious accident!' stormed Sancha.

Laughing hollowly, Zoe told her, 'You don't know the film business.'

'If it's that unreasonable I'm glad I don't! I don't know why you want to go on working for them.'

'Because I love making films, obviously! Why else would I be so keen to keep the job?'

Sancha typically switched attack, knowing she couldn't argue with that. 'The thing I couldn't understand was that you didn't have a car—how on earth did you get to work?'

'I took a taxi to a garage and hired a car, of course! Nothing difficult about that. I'd have thought you'd work it out for yourself.'

'Don't you talk to me as if I was a half-wit! I'm the sane one. I wouldn't risk my life going back to work the day after I nearly killed myself in a car! If you had any brains you'd have realised I'd be worried to death when I got back and found you gone.'

Zoe sighed, admitting the justice of the accusation. 'Yes, I know, I'm sorry if I worried you, Sancha, I didn't think of leaving a note. You're right, that's what I should have done, but I was in such a hurry. I'm okay, honestly—and there's no need for you to go over to my place…'

'Where are you ringing from?' Sancha's voice rose shrilly. 'Have you gone to work again?'

'Of course I have! I just explained—I can't afford to take any more time off!'

'Oh, for heaven's sake, Zoe, why are you so stupid? You just had a serious accident. Who knows what damage you did yourself? Sometimes it takes a day or two for an injury to show up. You should be in bed, not running about on a film set.'

Hastily, Zoe said, 'Sorry, Sancha—they're waiting for me to start shooting the next scene. Have to rush. Honestly, I didn't mean to upset you. Bye.'

As she slid her mobile phone into her bag she sighed with relief. She disliked being at odds with her sister over anything. They had always been so close; Sancha was her best friend, even if they didn't see eye to eye on all subjects. Men, for instance. Zoe had always felt Sancha was crazy, choosing a tough, domineering guy like Mark, marrying him, even forgiving him when Mark had showed signs of straying with some girl at his firm. Of course, Sancha swore there hadn't been anything serious between them. She said Mark had been faithful to her, had never slept with the other woman, and the intruder had gone now, was out of his life, married to someone else.

Maybe. But Mark had hurt Sancha, and Zoe, for one, found it hard to forgive him for that. Sancha had given him three wonderful children. Well, two wonderful boys—and Flora, the terrible. Spoilt, hyper, self-willed, it had been Flora who brought that marriage to the edge of disaster. She'd demanded all her mother's attention and had got it, which had meant that the boys and their father were left feeling shut out, abandoned, unloved.

Zoe could understand why Mark had been restless and tempted to stray, even though she didn't approve of it. He had apparently felt Sancha didn't love him any more, and, being the sort of man he was, very male, expecting attention from his woman all the time, that had made him smoulder with anger, hurt and resentment. So Sancha said. And no doubt she was right. It fitted everything Zoe knew about him.

All the same, Zoe knew she would never have trusted him again. Once he'd looked elsewhere, he might do so another time for another reason, she had told Sancha, but her sister had flared up.

'No! He won't, Zo. He loves me. He thought I no longer loved him, and he was hurt. I won't make the same mistake twice. From now on I'm going to make certain Mark is always sure I love him.'

A woman in love was a woman deluded, Zoe thought, joining Will. Well, not her! That wasn't happening to her. No man was blinding her to reason. She had never been that crazy about any man, and she had no intention of allowing love to take over her life the way it had her sister's.

By the time she got home that evening she was ready to drop, even though she hadn't worked very late. Normally she worked from sun-up until way into the night without this dragging sense of exhaustion, but her body obviously hadn't yet recovered from the shock of the accident. At least they were back on schedule, so the pressure was off, and she had broken as the sun dipped below the horizon, with the final scene she had had to shoot safely in the can. Then she had spent an hour talking to the crew about tomorrow's schedule before she'd got into her car and set off for her cottage.

Her nerves were jumping as she turned into her drive—after what had happened yesterday she was worried in case Larry was lurking there, waiting for her. Before she got out of her car she sat listening and looking around, but there were no movements, no sounds of any other human being in the garden, so she found her key, and with it firmly gripped in her hand, dived out of her car and ran to the front door, unlocked it and hurried inside.

After closing it behind her she leaned there, listening to the house. There were no threatening sounds, just the familiar, reassuring tick of clocks, the rustle of the wind outside. It was faintly chilly, but that was soon solved. Taking off her jacket, she hung it up before walking into the kitchen, where she switched on the central heating, then began to make herself a light supper of salad and thinly sliced chicken while she listened to her phone messages.

Sancha, scolding for a while, against a background of hammering and the tuneless moaning which was Flora singing. 'Darling, Mummy's talking to Aunty Zo, don't sing so loud,' Sancha said in the adoring way she always talked to Flora before switching to a normal voice to say to Zoe, 'We've been invited to a party Connel Hillier is giving this Saturday—will we see you there? We could give you a lift. Give me a ring this evening if you have time. Bye.'

Zoe poured herself a glass of dry white wine left over from a bottle Connel had opened yesterday. So he was giving a party was he? Well, when he got here she was going to tell him she wasn't going to his party; it would only give her sister ideas about them, ideas Zoe did not want Sancha to get.

Lifting the glass to her lips, she stiffened into stillness as his voice came out of the answer-machine, deep and urgent.

'Zoe, I have to go to London unexpectedly, so I won't see you this evening. Ring Sancha and she'll come over to spend the evening there, if you have any trouble. If that guy comes back, don't open the door, call the police.' A pause, then his voice dropped intimately, making pulses hammer at her wrists and neck. 'Goodnight, Zoe. See you.'

A click and he was gone, and she sat down, her legs wobbly under her. She wasn't a schoolgirl, for heaven's sake! Why should she feel disappointed just because he wasn't coming tonight? It was stupid. She didn't need him, or want him. She had lived alone for a long time; she was used to taking care of herself. She didn't need anybody.

She made herself start eating, drank her wine, cleared the table, loaded the dishwasher, then went up to bed, undressed rapidly, crawled between the covers and shut her eyes. She would not think about Connel. Images of him flickered like moths in the dark, but she resolutely ignored them.

Luckily, her weariness of mind and body meant she was soon asleep, a heavy, exhausted sleep; and if she dreamt she didn't remember it next morning.

The rest of that week went slowly by; she didn't hear from Connel again, but several times Sancha came to check up on her after she got back from work, scolding her about how tired she looked and how pale she was—was she having headaches? Wasn't she sleeping, was she eating?

'You have no sense!' she sighed one evening, shaking her head.

Zoe shook her head back. 'Stop worrying. I'm fine! Go home and take care of your kids, and stop hassling me!'

'No gratitude!' complained her sister. 'Look, I'll clear your supper things and start the dishwasher. Then, if you're sure you're okay, I'll get back.'

'You don't need to do anything, I'll manage,' Zoe said, but was told to sit down.

'It won't take me a minute.' A few minutes later the kitchen was spotless again. As she walked to the front door, Sancha asked, 'You are coming to Connel's party, aren't you?'

Trying not to sound as if she cared, Zoe said offhandedly, 'I haven't been invited!'

Looking surprised, Sancha said, 'He told us you'd be coming. He must have forgotten to ask you, just assumed you'd be there.'

'Typical of the man—always taking things for granted!'

'Shall I ring him and point out that he forgot to invite you?'

Going dark red, Zoe snapped, 'Don't you dare!'

Sancha smiled at her. 'Your problem is, you have too much pride! I know he meant to ask you—but he was called to London on urgent business and he's been there ever since. The party must have gone right out of his head.'

'Maybe he'll cancel it?'

'No, he talked to Mark this morning and said it was still on. He asked how you were, too.'

Trying to look indifferent, Zoe raised her brows. 'Oh?'

'That's one reason I came over this evening—Connel asked Mark if I was checking up on how you were.'

'And Mark said?'

'He said yes, and told me I'd better come over today because if you had died without anyone finding you, Connel might sack him.' The glint of amusement in Sancha's eyes made it clear she didn't mean that seriously.

Crossly amused, Zoe said, 'Oh, that's marvellous! And I thought you came because you loved me!'

Sancha grinned at her. 'You know I do. I'd have come anyway, if Mark hadn't insisted. I just thought you'd like to know Connel was still taking an interest in you.'

'Why should I care what he takes an interest in?'

Her sister gave her a wry look as she opened the front door, then shivered as a gust of cold night air hit her. 'There's a wind getting up; the weather's turning cold. It will be winter before we know it. Mark was talking about a skiing trip after Christmas—now that Flora's older we can take all the children. Why don't you come? We could all share one of those chalets with a maid— no housework or cooking for me, and the *après ski* is such fun.'

Zoe grimaced. 'With Flora around? Do me a favour.'

'She's growing up, Zoe! She's changing every day.

Playschool has made a big difference to her. She's learnt to share with other children and she doesn't have tantrums any more.'

Zoe looked disbelievingly at her sister and Sancha had the grace to laugh and admit, 'Well, not as often, anyway.'

'Only once or twice a day now, you mean?'

'No, once or twice a week! And when she does get into a tantrum it's nowhere near as earsplitting!' Sancha looked round with bright eyes. 'And Connel might come, too; Mark mentioned the idea to him and he seemed really keen. These chalets usually have half a dozen bedrooms so it works out cheaper for a big group of us to go.'

'Goodnight, Sancha,' Zoe said tersely, giving her a little push through the door.

'Think about it,' Sancha called, running to her car, her hair whipped into tangles by the wind.

Not answering, Zoe waved as her sister drove off, then thankfully shut the door on the chill of night and went up the stairs to bed.

Her sister was at her favourite game—matchmaking! For years she had been trying to find Zoe a husband. Why did married couples feel this urge to get their unmarried friends and relatives paired off? Presumably they couldn't stand to see other people free and happy!

Well, Sancha could forget it. No doubt it seemed a wonderful idea to match her with Mark's boss, but it wasn't going to happen. No way. Zoe didn't want to get married, for a start, and if she ever did so much as consider the idea the man would not be anything like Connel Hillier. He was exactly the type of guy she most disliked.

Interfering, domineering, high-handed, far too sure of himself, with the fixed idea that women were frail, delicate creatures who needed to be protected from themselves as well as other people.

True, he was more domesticated than she would ever have guessed he might be. She had to admit he could cook pretty well, and he was good at housework too. The man had depths to him she found surprising; he could be gentle, thoughtful, soothing. He had made an excellent nurse.

If she was honest, she would have to admit that she had missed him over the days since he went to London. He was good company, he made her laugh, which was something not many men did! And he's sexy, her conscience made her add. No denying that! That long, muscled body did something drastic to her heartbeat.

He's not just sexy, she thought. He's gorgeous, with those dark eyes, and that mouth...

Oh, stop it! she told herself, hurrying into the bathroom. She should be thinking about tomorrow's schedule, not Connel Hillier. Noisily splashing her face, she dwelt on what she would be shooting tomorrow.

Climbing into bed a few minutes later, she put out the light and yawned. What was Connel doing in London? she wondered, then caught herself at it and groaned aloud. She must stop thinking about that man. He turned up in her head far too often; it was time to evict him from her mind.

She dreamt about him instead.

In the morning as she was showering she tried to remember those dreams, but they had faded already. All she retained of them was a dim memory of Connel. It was probably just as well she had forgotten what he had been doing, she decided, viciously brushing her tangled red hair. And stop thinking about him! she told her flushed reflection.

By Friday her energy level was totally flat, and it began to show by lunchtime.

'Take the rest of the day off,' Will quietly said as they shared a tasteless cheese salad in her caravan. 'I can manage on my own this afternoon. You look as if you've reached the end of your rope.'

She put down the forkful of soapy cheese she had been about to put reluctantly into her mouth.

'Oh, Will, that would be such a relief!' Picking up her schedule, she considered the two short scenes they would be shooting later. There should be no problems in either of them for someone as experienced as Will. 'I must admit, I'm feeling terrible. My battery just ran out. If you're sure you don't mind?'

'Why should I mind? You know my ambition is to direct! I'd jump at the chance to practise! And, anyway, those two scenes are pretty straightforward. The actors know their words and their marks; we'll skate through them, no worries!'

She gave him a warm hug. 'You're a real mate! Thanks, Will.' Before leaving, she spoke to the rest of the crew and the actors; nobody voiced any objections to Will taking over. Ten minutes later she was on her way home.

It was a cold, bright day, troubled only by gusts of wind. Gutters at the side of the roads were filling up with russet, brown and orange leaves from the stripping trees, which tossed and swayed like dancers, while curls of blue-grey smoke twisted up from the gardens of cottages, giving a nostalgic scent to the autumn air. It was a pity to spend a day like this in bed, but Zoe was too tired to do anything else.

On reaching her cottage she read her post, discovered there were no messages on her answer-machine, made herself a cup of tea and a slice of toast and peanut butter, took them up to bed with her, took off her jeans and shirt and got between the sheets. She ate her toast, drank her tea, yawning, with heavy lids, then gratefully lay down and five minutes later was fast asleep.

It seemed seconds later when she was woken up by a loud, persistent ringing.

Heart thumping, flushed and off balance, Zoe sat up, believing at first that the noise was her alarm going off and reaching to switch it off only to realise as she took hold of the clock that the sound came from elsewhere. From downstairs, in fact.

It was now dark outside; looking at the green-glowing hands of the clock she was startled to see it was nine in the evening— she must have slept for six hours! And someone was ringing her doorbell.

Who would come visiting at this time of night? Sancha? The ringing was still just as shrill, just as insistent. She stumbled out of bed, ran to the window and looked out. It wasn't her sister. That was a man, tall and unmistakably male in jeans and a sweater.

Not Larry? she thought, heart sinking. She hadn't heard from or seen him since the last time he was here. Optimistically she had begun to believe she would never be bothered by him again.

She opened the window, and at the sound of the latch

grating backwards the tall, dark figure at the front door stepped back at the sound of the window being opened wide and stared up at her.

Moonlight fell on Connel's face, carving strange, shifting patterns across the familiar angles of cheeks and nose, mouth and temples, making his black hair silver, glittering in his eyes.

Breathless and weak with excitement, Zoe clutched the windowsill for support.

'Are you naked?' Connel asked, shattering her mood in an instant.

'No, I'm not!' she crossly denied. Not quite, anyway. 'I was in bed, as it happens. What are you doing here at this hour?'

'I just got back from London so I came to see how you are.'

'I was fine until you woke me up!'

'Sorry, I expected you to be up because I could see lights on downstairs in your kitchen.'

'Lights? I didn't put any lights on. I wonder if Sancha has come round?' Zoe turned and Connel urgently called out to her.

'Wait! Don't go down there; you could have burglars. If it was Sancha I'd see her car out here, and I don't. It could be your ex-boyfriend and we know he's violent. Chuck me down your key and I'll let myself in and deal with whoever it is.'

Zoe hesitated, but it was common sense to do as he said, so she looked in her handbag, found her front door key and threw it down. As Connel began to open the door she hurried to dress in her jeans and sweater, pulled a hairbrush over her hair, and was on the small landing at the turn of the stairs when she met Connel coming up.

'Where are you going?' she sharply asked as he ran an all-seeing gaze over her.

'To check the upstairs rooms—there was nobody on the ground floor.' He looked up into her eyes. 'You got dressed.'

Ignoring the comment, pink and suspicious, she demanded, 'How do I know there were lights on in the kitchen before you got into the cottage? I didn't see them, I only have your word for it, and as I came home in daylight I certainly didn't switch on any lights.'

Coolly, he told her, 'There's a note from your sister propped up on the table—she came round at six, found you asleep and tiptoed off again. Now, let me pass and I'll just look in the rooms up here. There's no point in not making sure nobody has got in, is there?'

She stepped sideways, squashing herself against the wall to let him pass. As he joined her on the narrow landing their bodies almost touched; Zoe was abruptly deafened by the violent racing of her blood in her ears and her pulses everywhere else, in her throat, at her wrists, deep inside her body. She had never been so physically aware of anyone in her life and it scared her, scared her senseless.

She couldn't meet his eyes, looked downwards, but through her drooping lashes watched him, taller than ever in black jeans and a dark grey silky cashmere sweater which clung to his strong chest. His was an intensely physical presence, making her body clamour and her senses burn.

He made no move to go on up the stairs. Instead, he

leaned slowly towards her, as if in slow motion, giving
her plenty of time to escape, a chance she could not take
because his deliberate, almost taunting, slowness made
her mouth dry and chained her to the spot. Connel put
both hands on the wall on either side of her, and softly
asked, 'Missed me?'

Her breathing seemed to stop, as if she had died; desperately she snatched at air, refusing to let him send her
into this spiral of desire and panic and helplessness. No
man had ever done this to her. She wasn't going to let
Connel Hillier drown her mind and bewilder her body.

Hoarsely, she lied, 'I've been too busy to miss anybody! Have you been away? Anywhere exciting?'

He put a finger under her chin and tipped her head
back before she could stop him, forcing her to look up
into those mocking, narrowed eyes.

'What a spiky little hedgehog you are, aren't you?
Every time I try to get any closer, you roll yourself up
into a ball and I find myself impaled on your sharp prick-
les.'

'Better stay away from me then, hadn't you?' she
breathlessly whispered, fighting not to stare at his mouth.
Why did it have this hypnotic attraction for her? Okay,
it was beautifully shaped, but so what? In her job, she
met terrific-looking actors with sexy mouths every day.
Not one of them had ever had this irresistible lure! In
fact, if asked, she would have said she was immune to
good-looking men. Some of them she positively disliked
because their looks made then vain; some of them were
as thick as fog. Look at Hal Thaxford! For her a man
needed a lot of other qualities—a sense of humour, kind-
ness, honesty, brains, integrity, common sense. If he was

attractive physically too, great, but looks weren't a vital part of the package for her. So why couldn't she stop gazing at Connel like some star-struck kid?

He took a step closer, so that their bodies almost touched. 'I gather that despite everything the doctor said, you've worked every day. Mark told me his wife was very worried about it.'

Her eyes flashed. Mark had no business discussing her with him! 'I'm fine,' she said crossly. 'Look, are you going upstairs or not? Because if you're not, let me pass. I want to go and make some coffee and something to eat.'

'Do you know what I want?' he whispered, and her heart turned over.

'No!' she lied, slid under his barring arm and began to hurry downstairs, only to have her feet skid underneath her.

Gasping, she found herself tumbling forward and reached for the banister, but in the same second Connel caught her by the waist and yanked her back upwards.

Instinctively, Zoe clung to him, still off balance, trembling, realising how nearly she had fallen down the steep stairs.

'You're the most accident-prone female I ever met,' Connel muttered, his lips brushing the pink, whorled folds of her ear, sending shivers down her spine.

She hadn't been, until she met him, but she wasn't telling him so; the admission was far too betraying. He had disrupted her entire life since the minute they met. At times she even wondered if her immediate uneasiness and distrust when first setting eyes on him hadn't been

her instincts warning her, telling her he could be trouble
and she would be well-advised to steer clear of him.

Her whole body jerked in shock at that instant as
Connel's mouth began wandering down her throat, a
warm, gentle exploration which frightened her because
she liked it far too much.

'Stop that!' She pulled her head back but that didn't
stop him; it merely gave him further to travel along her
exposed throat. His mouth reached her sweater neckline
and nuzzled it back to let him kiss her shoulders, and
lower to the smooth rise of her breasts.

Zoe grabbed his thick black hair to drag his head
away. 'No!'

His face was very close; she stared into his dark, glittering eyes. 'No!' she said again.

'Yes,' he breathed, then his mouth closed over hers,
and Zoe was swallowed up in a wave of fierce pleasure.
There was suddenly no distance between them at all.
Connel's body touched hers from shoulder to knee; you
couldn't have got a piece of paper between them. His
arms clamped her to him so tightly she could only just
breathe. His mouth had forced her lips apart, or had she
simply opened her mouth without knowing what she was
doing? Probably. She was out of control; she couldn't
deny it. She wasn't some helpless victim. She wasn't
fighting him off. No.

She was kissing him back. Groaning. Was that her
voice, moaning as if she was drowning far out? Was that
her saying his name over and over again?

Connel. Connel. Connel. That was her voice, wasn't
it?

His hands were wandering up and down her back, as

if playing music on her spine. She trembled, sighing. Yes, Yes, Yes.

Was she saying it aloud or just thinking...

Yes, kiss me...touch me...Connel, yes.

One of his hand slid caressingly down over her slim buttocks in the tight jeans, taking all the time in the world, while the other took hold of her waist.

She didn't understand what he was doing until she realised she was being lifted off the ground and carried. Not downstairs. Back upstairs. To her bedroom.

That woke her up, fast. She began kicking, pummelling him; startling him so much he dropped her before he reached the bed.

Glaring, Zoe faced him, hands screwed into fists, eyes hard. 'Oh, no, you don't, mister! I'm not that easy. Get out of my house, and I mean now!'

He stood there, measuring her thoughtfully, feet apart, poised as if for a fight.

'What changed your mind?'

'Just go, will you?'

'You were saying yes a minute ago.'

'No!'

'You said yes. Not just once, either, over and over again!' His eyes gleamed at her, sensual enjoyment in them. She knew what he was remembering, she was remembering it, too, but she wished she could forget what she had said, how she had kissed him back.

Angrily she broke out, 'Look, I've had enough of this argument—will you please leave?'

'Not yet. I want you to admit how you felt. You know you were giving me a green light.'

She threw caution to the winds. Chin up, she defiantly muttered, 'Well, I changed my mind!'

His mouth twisted ironically. 'Well, at least you admit it now. You told me you were prone to changing your mind about men—I had no idea you did it so fast. One minute you were as hot as fire. The next you turned into a wild cat. Why, Zoe? What changed your mind?'

She hesitated, then decided to be completely frank. 'You went too fast. I hardly know you and I don't believe in sleeping with strange men. I may have dated a lot of guys, but I rarely sleep with them. These days, it's asking for trouble. I don't believe in sleeping with a man on the first date. Or the second or third, come to that. I don't believe in promiscuity, full stop. I'm terrified of getting Aids or some other sexual disease. I like to know the man pretty well before I risk my life on him, and I don't know much about you, do I?'

He went on watching her, his face coolly unreadable, but she heard him breathing rapidly, thickly, as if he had just run a marathon. 'Okay, I take your point. Same here, in fact. I'm not promiscuous either, for much the same reasons.'

Her green eyes flashed at him. 'Yet you tried it on with me just now! How can I believe a word you say when you tell me one thing and do another?'

He grimaced. 'You're right, of course. It was reckless and stupid.' His voice dropped, deepened, his breathing still rough and uneven. 'You went to my head, Zoe. I lost control. Don't you know how sexy you were when we were kissing? You suddenly seemed to have no bones, and you were making the sexiest noises. You were white-hot, and you turned me on.'

She was hot again right now, her face burning, her body shaking as if in fever. She yelled at him in shame and humiliation. 'Shut up. Shut up, will you? I don't want to talk about it any more. I just want you to get out of my house and leave me alone!' She ran over to her mobile, which lay on the bedside table, picked it up and began clicking in numbers. 'I'm calling the police. You've got ten seconds to get out of here.'

For a second she thought he was going to defy her and stay, go on arguing, but after giving her a long, hard stare she could not decipher he turned on his heel and walked out without another word.

She heard him go down the stairs, heard him slam out of the house. Standing by the window, she watched him drive away, his tail-lights winking red as he disappeared down the drive and out into the lane beyond.

Only then did she break down, burst into tears. Connel had got too close, emotionally and physically. He had come close to taking off her clothes and entering her. She had come close to letting him do whatever he liked. She had wanted him—with a need that was almost pain.

Now she felt grief, an aching loss, as if something world-shattering, something explosively important, had almost happened to her, then at the last minute been snatched away.

It had been her decision. She had stopped him. So why did she feel guilty? Why was she standing here with tears running down her face?

It was time she made up her mind—how did she really feel about Connel Hillier?

CHAPTER EIGHT

NEXT morning she got up late, enjoying even more than usual the pleasure of being able to stay in bed as long as she liked. After a breakfast of porridge cooked in the microwave, which made life so much simpler than having to cook it in a saucepan and keep stirring it to make sure it didn't burn, she went shopping and had coffee in the village pub, The White Swan, which was no longer the sole haunt of men but had become something of a meeting place for both sexes, and all ages. This social revolution meant that she had found the bar packed with other women who had done their weekend shopping and were now sitting together, gossiping and having coffee; some of them eating hot croissants or toast, too. Some of them had children with them—if food was being eaten children were allowed in the bar, but had to leave once food was no longer served. The arrival of women in pubs had brought about a big improvement in decor. Carpets on the floor, where once there had been sawdust, comfortable couches instead of wooden benches, bright colour schemes and ornaments and pictures on the walls.

It was a bright, cold day; Zoe sat in a windowseat so that she could gaze out at the little garden running beside the pub. There were few flowers around at this late date in autumn, and the deciduous trees might be almost leafless, but a holly tree still had its dark green leaves, and was also covered in scarlet berries. Country people said

that meant a hard winter ahead. Nature provided food
for birds in bad weather when the ground was too frozen
for them to find insects easily.

There were other bushes in flower: a Viburnum shrub
covered in pink flowers, some white winter-flowering
roses, a few orange chrysanthemums and some rather
scrubby-looking purple Michaelmas daisies. Those
splashes of colour lifted Zoe's spirits, which had been
rather low from the minute she got up and remembered
what had happened yesterday.

She was depressed. Oh, not because Connel had made
that pass. Men were always doing that. She coped with
them casually, easily. She didn't resent passes—in some
ways they were flattering, so long as they could be
fended off without trouble. When someone weird like
Larry made a pass it could be scary, of course, because
he wouldn't give up, he turned nasty when you rejected
him, but most men took no for an answer and backed
off.

Last night she hadn't been afraid Connel might be
dangerous, might try force or turn nasty. That wasn't
what was worrying her, dragging her spirits down.

The trouble was, she had wanted him, even though
she had said no. For the first time in her life she had
really wanted a man so badly that it had been very hard
to stop him, and she wasn't sure what that meant.

In fact, she was confused, bewildered, uneasy, her
thoughts went round and round in circles whenever she
tried to think it all out, but worst of all her brain appeared to turn to melting ice cream the instant images
of Connel entered her head.

Am I in love? she wondered one minute, then the next

angrily thought, No! Of course she wasn't. In love! The very idea made her laugh.

Except, of course, that it didn't. Because she wasn't laughing. She was far too depressed even to smile.

Some Saturdays she had lunch out, met neighbours and friends and chatted to them, but today she wasn't staying here for lunch with the regulars. She decided to have cheese, salad and a slab of French bread at home instead, so she headed for her cottage after leaving the pub.

While she was unpacking her groceries she switched on the answer-machine.

'Hallo, Zoe.' Connel's voice made her start so violently that she dropped a box of eggs on the floor.

'Damn, damn, damn,' Zoe muttered, looking down at the mess. Luckily, her kitchen floor was tiled and easy to clean, but even so what a nuisance to have that to clear up!

Connel's voice was deep and husky. 'I'm sorry about last night. Can we start again? I'm having a party this evening—Mark and Sancha are coming. Will you come with them? Please, Zoe.'

His voice vanished, the machine switched off, and Zoe leaned on the kitchen wall, breathless.

Should she go?

No. Not on your life. Only an idiot would risk seeing him again; she was staying away from him in future.

She looked at her reflection in the chrome fitting of the oven: green eyes huge and glowing, with dilated pupils; face flushed, mouth parted and trembling. Who do you think you're kidding? she asked her mirror image.

Wild horses couldn't drag you away from the chance to see him again.

You're hooked, addicted. A sad case. Hadn't she always despised women who got themselves into this state of hopeless dependence on one man? Well, now she could despise herself.

She turned away and set about clearing up the broken eggs before she finished unpacking the groceries.

A quarter of an hour later, while she was eating her cheese, French bread, and salad, Sancha rang, her brisk voice making it clear she was in a combative mood. 'Are you coming tonight or not?'

'I suppose so,' Zoe reluctantly said.

Her sister spluttered. 'You're very annoying, do you know that? This is a party—not a visit to the dentist! You might try to sound as if you expected to enjoy yourself!'

Meekly, Zoe sighed. 'Sorry. I'm eating my lunch and thinking about work…'

'What else do you ever think about?' Sancha accused.

Wouldn't you love it if you knew? thought Zoe, but said aloud, 'What should I wear?'

'Mark told me to put on something pretty, not just casual clothes. Not jeans, in other words. It isn't a barbecue, although there is a well-lit garden we can explore, apparently. But there's a caterer doing the food. Mark says some important clients will be there, people Connel wants to impress. Mostly rich people, I gather, who'll be dressed up to kill, so take a lot of trouble to look your best, Zoe, for Mark's sake!'

'A dress, then, not jeans?' It sounded rather boring, though. Rich businessmen *en masse* were not her favourite people. She never knew what to say to them. They led such tedious lives.

'Of course—I told you, no jeans! We'll pick you up at seven-fifteen. Okay?'

After she had rung off Zoe sat down to sip the glass of apple juice she was drinking with her meal. Only then did it occur to her to wonder where Connel lived. A flutter of excitement began in her stomach. What sort of place did he have? She was curious.

Let's face it, she was curious about everything to do with Connel. His background, his family, where he lived, what he read, what he did in his spare time! Any detail about him was interesting to her.

She began impatiently clearing away the evidence of her meal. Couldn't she think of something else? That afternoon she worked on next week's film schedule, noting down new ideas for scenes, frowning over the script and worksheet.

At six she went upstairs to have a shower before getting dressed. After putting on filmy black silk bra and panties, richly trimmed with lace, then a matching black chemise, with a deep band of lace at the hem and neck, she wriggled into a very brief black dress. Armless and almost backless, it began just where her breasts began, leaving a tantalising glimpse of white flesh, then clung all the way down to just above her knees, so tight it was a second skin.

Staring at herself in it, she hesitated—was it too daring for a private party? She had bought it to wear on public occasions, film functions, award ceremonies, times when she would be on view, when the paparazzi would be swarming and reporters around. It was a dress to dazzle, to catch the eye, make people look twice, maybe three or four times. It was a dress to be seen in!

She had only worn it once or twice before, and she knew it was not a dress you could relax in. Men stared too much, especially if you forgot and bent forward even a little so that they saw more of your breasts.

Should she change into something less daring? She looked at her watch, groaning. No, there was no time; it was seven now and Mark and Sancha would arrive before she got her make-up on if she didn't hurry.

Cautiously perching on the edge of her dressing-table stool, she began to smooth foundation over her skin with her fingertips.

As she had suspected, her sister and brother-in-law arrived promptly. Hearing their car grate over the gravel, Zoe took a last look at herself, grimaced, then fled, grabbing up her black velvet cape and black velvet evening bag from the bed as she ran.

When she opened the front door there was a silence, then Mark gave a long wolf whistle, his brows rising.

Sancha said, 'That dress is…' Words appeared to fail her for a second, then she took a long breath and said, 'I've never seen you wear it before—did you buy it specially for tonight? It will certainly make Connel sit up.'

'And beg,' Mark dryly murmured.

'I didn't dress for Connel Hillier,' snapped Zoe. 'And it isn't new. It's the dress I bought in the spring, when we were up for a Best New Feature Film award, which we should have won, but which was stolen from us by…'

Sancha's eyes widened and she interrupted. 'Oh, yes,

I remember! I caught a glimpse of it while we were watching the television news coverage of the awards.'

'I wasn't on the TV programme! As we didn't win, they weren't interested in us,' Zoe bitterly said.

'No, but when they announced the nominees for that category they scanned the tables of each film up for the award, and I saw you, with the rest of the people in your film, the actors, and Will, and your assistant, whatever her name is...but as you were sitting down I didn't realise the dress was so...'

Her voice tailed off.

'So what?' demanded Zoe, bristling. 'What's wrong with this dress?'

'Not a thing,' Mark said, grinning wickedly, looking her up and down, from her wild red hair to her creamy, naked shoulders and the smoothness of her half-covered breasts, down over the tight black dress to her long, sleek legs and small feet in expensive Italian black leather high heels. 'It's scrumptious, positively delicious. You'll be fighting men off all evening.'

'Would you like me to get one just like it?' Sancha asked in a chilly voice.

'You? Certainly not,' he said, frowning. 'You're my wife, a respectable married woman—I don't want other men eying you in public, and if you wore that dress they would.'

Sancha looked at Zoe. 'Now do you see what I mean?'

'I see your husband has two standards—one for you and one for other women. And if I were you I wouldn't be pleased about that! Unless you have the harem mentality,' Zoe tartly said. 'Look, are we going to this party or not?'

'Temper, temper,' Mark said, laughing.

'What do you mean, harem mentality?' Sancha asked indignantly.

Without answering Zoe switched off the hall light, closed her front door and stalked, head held high, to their car.

'I understand what Mark means,' her sister said, following. 'I wouldn't want other women staring at him, either.'

'Jealousy is childish,' Zoe said, getting into the car.

'Oh, of course, you wouldn't be jealous if you saw your man with someone else!' Sancha snapped.

'No, I'd just dump him and walk away without a backward glance.'

'That's what you always do anyway!'

'If you two keep squabbling you won't enjoy the party,' Mark told them as he got behind the wheel.

Zoe had just remembered that last year Mark had been involved with someone else, and Sancha had been very hurt, jealous, unhappy, but had refused to leave him, had fought like a tiger for her marriage. How could I forget that? Zoe asked herself. How stupid can you be? She couldn't apologise, either, in front of Mark, so she lapsed into silence and stared out of the window as he drove off, along the lane, back to the main road, where he drove across into another lane which led to the village of Rookby, half a dozen miles away. After driving along the main street, lined on each side by small pastel-washed cottages in terraces, with a few older buildings scattered between them, a lurching black and white Tudor house, a couple of white-plastered, bow-fronted eighteenth-century houses, Mark turned left by the old church.

That was medieval, with a rather squat bell tower and stone and flint walls, surrounded by a green sea of grass lapping at old gravestones. The lane wandered on for five minutes until they reached some tall, white gates. Mark spun through them and slowly proceeded up a wide drive fringed by silver birch trees which gleamed strangely, like slender ghosts, in the light of tall black-painted lamps set at intervals. Suddenly through the trees they saw the house, a square black shape against the starry sky, windows glinting at them.

'Is that his house?' Sancha gasped. 'It looks huge.'

'No, but it is quite large—six bedrooms, a stable block behind it—and it's early Georgian, built around 1760,' Mark told her. 'It was very run-down when Connel bought it, needed a new roof, a lot of replastering, central heating put in. It was damp in some of the rooms. It took him about a year to put it all right, and for the last year he's been having it redecorated, inside and out; Connel got in a very classy firm who did the lot, found furniture, chose colour schemes, advised on carpets. He didn't have time to do all that himself. But now it's finished and he's pleased with the way the place looks— hence the party, this is a sort of house-warming.'

Sancha sighed wistfully. 'I'd love to live in a place like this!'

'So would I,' Mark dryly said. 'But I'm afraid I'm not in Connel's income bracket, love, so unless you divorce me and marry Connel, you never will.'

'I'll think about it,' Sancha said, giggling. 'To own a house like this he must be very rich.'

'Very,' Mark said, sliding a glance at Zoe over his shoulder. 'You're very quiet, Zoe. Seeing Connel in a new light, are you?'

'I was thinking about the work involved in running a place as big as this,' she coolly said. 'All those rooms to keep clean!'

'Connel has a housekeeper who cooks for him, several part-time cleaners, and a gardener.'

Staring, as they came closer and she could see the house more clearly, the rows of pedimented windows, the high-pitched red roof, the elegance of the structure, Zoe said, 'His wife would spend hours every day just organising the staff!'

Mark gave her another wry look, brows lifting. 'Determined not to be impressed, Zoe?'

A little angry colour stole into her face, but she was saved the necessity of replying because he was just pulling up outside the façade of the house in a large parking bay to the side of the front door. There was only just room for their car; a couple of dozen cars were parked echelon-style already.

This was obviously quite a large party, thought Zoe, as she and Sancha got out. While Mark was locking his car Zoe whispered to her sister, 'Sorry I snapped earlier.'

She got a wry, sideways smile. 'That's okay, I forgive you. I always do, don't I? Are you nervous, Zo?'

'Nervous?'

'About seeing Connel again?'

'Of course not!' She flushed crossly, but knew her sister had come close to the truth—she was edgy about seeing Connel.

He had had a dangerous effect on her. It was hard to

admit that, especially as she had no idea how to cope with her feelings.

Mark caught up with them and they walked on in silence towards the white portico of the front door, feet crunching on the gravel. In spite of the cloudless sky, the stars, the night air was quite warm, yet Zoe was shivering inside her velvet cloak. Seeing this beautiful home had altered her perception of Connel.

She had begun to think of him the way she thought of men she worked with: colleagues, comrades, men you could talk to, casually, as a friend, men you could trust and rely on.

The way he had cooked for her, taken care of her, tidied up and cleaned the house, had not prepared her for what she saw now. Connel did not cook for himself; Mark had just told her. He did not clean his own home. He had servants to do all that for him. Connel, in fact, lived in a different world from her. They had nothing in common. Zoe felt oddly depressed by that thought.

A grey-haired, middle-aged woman, wearing a neat black dress, opened the front door and smiled at them, ushered them into an oak-panelled hall, took their coats and showed them into a long, elegantly furnished room filled with people whose voices made the room seem much smaller than it was; Zoe didn't recognise a single face.

A girl, also in black, offered a tray of drinks. Zoe took Buck's Fizz, orange juice spiked with champagne. So did Sancha. Together they stood, staring around.

The room was classically decorated; the walls painted a smooth, soft eggshell-blue; the white ceiling elaborately plastered, with swags of flowers, cherubs, in the centre of which a chandelier swung, Venetian glass dripping down from rows of bud-like bulbs. There were dark blue velvet sofas here and there, and matching chairs scattered along the walls, leading towards a well-lit garden you could see through open French windows hung with floor-length curtains in the same shade.

'What do you think of the decor?' Sancha whispered, and Zoe shrugged.

'No surprises, are there? I mean, the colour choice and the decor are conventional, traditional, what you would expect in a house like this.'

'But it is so elegant,' Sancha wistfully said.

'If you like that sort of thing.' Zoe gave her a teasing look. 'Just imagine Flora in this room, chucking toys about, not to mention her lunch! How elegant would it look after Flora got to it?'

In the middle of sipping her Buck's Fizz, Sancha snorted with amusement, then began to cough. Zoe slapped her on the back.

'Are you okay?'

'The drink went up my nose!'

'Flora gets up my nose!' Zoe laughed, then stopped as she saw Connel, across the room, in profile. Something disastrous happened to her heartbeat. If she had been drinking her Buck's Fizz at that instant she might have choked, too.

Sancha's eyes followed the direction of her gaze. 'Doesn't he look gorgeous?'

Without replying Zoe agreed, absorbing with her eyes and heart what he was wearing: an elegant dark wool suit, beautifully cut and fitting him like a glove, with a waistcoat which emphasised his slim waist, a crisp white shirt and a dark red silk tie. Yes. He looked gorgeous; even sexier than usual. She remembered the sinister, brooding look he had had the night they met in the rain, and smiled to herself. You wouldn't know it was the same man, would you?

Her gaze travelled on to the woman with him, her face raised towards Connel's, her blue eyes smiling into his. 'Who's that he's talking to?' she asked her sister flatly and, she hoped, unrevealingly.

'I've no idea,' Sancha slowly told her. 'She's...pretty, isn't she?'

'Pretty' was hardly the word. The woman was riveting a lot of men's eyes and no wonder. Slender, with a smooth, perfect, golden tanned skin, blonde hair swept up into a chignon, she was wearing white, a sort of Grecian goddess dress, clinging to her in soft silky folds from halfway down her breasts, cascading down her body to her feet.

'How does it stay up?' muttered Sancha.

'Will-power,' Zoe coldly said. She looked as if she had lots of that. Her pink mouth smiled widely, but there was determination in her beautiful face and in every angle of those glittering blue eyes, the perfect butterfly mouth, the rather formidable jaw.

'I wonder who she is?' Sancha thought aloud.

'Maybe she works for him?' They seemed to know each other pretty well. Maybe they were lovers? Or had been?

There was an intimacy in the way the girl looked at him that suggested they were more than acquaintances. Zoe's throat felt as if she had just swallowed broken glass. Unlike Larry, Connel hadn't insisted on telling her about his past love life. He hadn't mentioned other women at all. Somehow she had got the impression he wasn't seeing anyone, and as he had been abroad, on this exploration trip, for a year, she had assumed there hadn't been anyone all that time.

'She's Bianca Green,' said Mark, joining them, an amused look on his face, as if he had been eavesdropping before they'd noticed him. 'She's the interior designer who did the house. Looks as if you've got competition, Zoe.'

She gave him a disdainful glance. 'I never compete for men!' On an afterthought, she added, 'And I'm not interested in Connel Hillier, anyway,' and hoped her face and voice were convincing.

'Oh? I had the idea you sounded a trifle jealous!' mocked Mark, and her teeth met.

'No,' she said through them, but the word emerged squashed and rather forced.

'Sure?' asked Mark, and actually laughed.

She glared. 'Quite sure, thanks!'

'Well, I certainly suspect Bianca has her eye on Connel. She's clever and ambitious, but it isn't easy to make money in her business. She needs backing, someone with money behind her.' Mark grinned. 'Of course, she could fancy Connel, too. No doubt she does. Very convenient, falling for someone who is just the backer she needs, but then I have the feeling Bianca would be lucky that way.'

Yes, Zoe had that feeling, too. She had taken an instant dislike to the blonde woman with that beautiful, enamelled, hard-baked face. But she didn't want to give Mark any more reasons for teasing her, so she looked away, as if bored, and was relieved to spot Hal Thaxford on the other side of the room.

He was wearing an unbelievably over-the-top red velvet jacket, a frilly white silk shirt, a red velvet cummerbund and black satin trousers which made him look like a band leader from the nineteen thirties, although Hal probably meant to look like a top sex symbol. He was chatting up a wide-eyed girl of about nineteen, who clearly thought he was God's gift to women. So did Hal, of course. Most of his fans were either teenagers or middle-aged women. Anybody with any brains and experience saw past the dark, brooding façade to the dummy underneath.

'Excuse me, there's Hal. I must talk to him about work,' Zoe coolly informed her sister and Mark, and walked off, keeping her eyes averted from the sight of Connel flirting with the blonde harpy.

As Hal saw her coming he took on a wary, uneasy look. He had learnt to expect trouble from her on a film set and they were about to work together again, unless she was coming over to tell him she was dropping him.

'Oh, hi, Zoe.'

She smiled brightly, and he flinched, not used to smiles like that from her and immediately expecting the worst.

'Sorry to interrupt, Hal, but I want to talk to you about work.' She turned her smile on the girl, who visibly hated her. 'Would you mind giving us a few minutes alone?'

'This is Zoe. She's directing me in a film next week,' Hal told the girl, making it sound as if he was the star instead of just playing a small part. 'Zoe, this is Cherie Lewin. She's at drama school.'

And wearing what looked like a deckchair, thought Zoe, still smiling. What gave the poor girl the idea that a tunic dress striped in bright yellow and green would do anything for her?

'An actress? Which school are you at?'

The girl told her, staring back and bitterly absorbing the way Zoe's black dress revealed her figure.

'I'll look out for you when you leave school. I like to use new talent,' Zoe said, trying to be kind, although privately feeling the girl had all the charisma and sparkle of a dead lightbulb. Then, turning to Hal, she slid her hand through his arm and drew him away. 'We'll go into the garden and get some air, shall we, Hal? It's a lovely night.'

She headed for the French windows and he went with her meekly, saying over his shoulder, 'See you later, Cherie.'

The paths were well lit by Victorian standard lamps set at intervals, almost turning night into day out there. There was a faint scent of roses from a sunken garden built in the centre of a wide lawn; Zoe wandered towards the red brick steps leading down into it, inhaling the perfume of the roses.

'I thought roses only bloomed in summer; these are flowering late,' Hal said, bending towards a white standard rose-bush in a graceful pose she recognised as that of an actor trying to impress a director. Hal was always conscious of what he looked like. His body was one of the tools of his trade; he took care of it, loved and cherished it.

'I sometimes have roses in bloom in December, in my garden,' Zoe told him. 'It depends on the type of rose you plant. Some are early, some are late. You can have roses throughout the year if you buy the right ones.' She walked on, staring around her. 'This looks like an old rose garden to me—there's so much moss growing on these brick walls. Maybe it's Victorian. They were very keen on sunken rose gardens.'

'They're very romantic, aren't they? A great place for lovers to meet.'

Zoe's eyes narrowed. 'Hey! You've given me a terrific idea. There's a very romantic scene in the film...'

'The one between me and Lindsay?' Hal's interest, as always, brightened when anyone talked about him.

Nodding, she murmured, 'A sunken rose garden would make a great setting for that scene, don't you think? Just imagine it.'

'Wow. Yeah,' said Hal breathlessly, imagining like mad as far as his own part was concerned. 'I could kiss her hand...that always gets the women...'

Zoe gave him a look through her eyelashes. He was so transparent. 'Do you think you could persuade your cousin to lend us this garden for a day? That's all it would take. The scene is only a couple of minutes, but the setting makes all the difference. You and Lindsay could sit on that seat over there—behind you the climbing roses on the pergola... It would be perfect, don't you think?'

'Oh, yeah, I can see it now.' Hal gazed at her, sighing. 'Hey, I just noticed—in that dress you look wonderful, really sexy, Zoe. You should have been an actress yourself, you know.'

She opened her eyes wider. 'Me? An actress?' Was he kidding? Who would rather be an actress than a director? Who would rather be a doll than a dollmaker? 'I couldn't...I can't act.'

'You wouldn't need to, looking the way you do.' Hal's eyes ate her, from her bare shoulders down over the clinging dress to her long, slim legs. Time to change the subject, she decided. She didn't want to have problems with Hal Thaxford.

'Could you talk to Connel tonight?' she pleaded, fluttering her lashes. 'While he's in a good mood, get it fixed up? I'll bring the scene forward so we can do it here on Tuesday.'

'Yeah, sure, I'll talk to him.'

'Good boy,' Zoe said, in the warm, firm tones she might use to an obedient dog, and turned to hurry away before he tried to take liberties. Unfortunately, in her hurry, on those delicate high heels, she tripped on slippery paving stones.

Hal jumped to catch her. 'Steady!'

She looked up, laughing. 'Thanks, Hal. Apparently I'm accident-prone, ever since my car crash. I never was before.'

'Maybe the crash had a psychological effect on you?' Hal seriously suggested, still holding her by the waist. 'Made you nervous, so you keep having accidents?'

'Maybe,' she said, wondering if he had hit a nail on the head. Then she felt his hand sliding up her spine and had the strong suspicion he was about to make a pass. Just as she was about to move away from him a chill voice from the brick steps behind them made them both start.

'Rehearsing? Or is this romantic scene for real?'

CHAPTER NINE

HAL let go of her and spun round, relaxing with a grin as he recognised his cousin. 'Oh, hi, Connel—we were just talking about you!'

'Oh, were you?' Connel drawled, staring fixedly at Zoe, those hard, glittering dark eyes sliding over her red hair, faintly dishevelled by the night air and by almost falling over. His gaze moved on to study her full red mouth, like a policeman looking for evidence—of what? she thought—before travelling slowly, with invasive intensity, over her body in the black dress as if he could see her naked.

She felt her throat flutter with awareness and nerves; now he looked the way he had the night they met in the rain: dangerous, sinister, smouldering. He was obviously angry—but why? What was he thinking, staring at her like that? His eyes accused, as if she had committed a crime.

'I didn't notice you doing any talking,' he bit out. 'I got a very different impression of what you were doing.'

Hal looked flattered, preening like an idiot parrot. His conceit was incredible. He probably believed he had cracked her at last; she was falling for him, the way so many women did! Zoe could have hit him.

She wasn't flattered. She was insulted. Did Connel really think she had been flirting with Hal, inviting him to make a pass at her? After everything she had said about the man?

'You were right the first rime,' she coldly said. 'We were talking about work.'

'Oh, sure you were! How could I have thought otherwise? Of you of all people! As if you'd be out here in the moonlight...' He paused, his mouth cynical, and looked her up and down again. 'In that dress...' he enlarged, making it sound like an insult, 'doing anything but talk about work!'

She went scarlet with rage. 'It's the truth! I had an idea for a scene Hal's going to be doing next week! I'll leave him to explain. I might hit you if I stayed here.'

She walked off before either man could stop her, but all the way back to the house she could feel Connel's hostile eyes boring their way through her back. Well, it had been a great idea to shoot that scene in his garden, it would have lifted the whole film, and it often gave a film more depth to have a wide variety of backgrounds, but he would probably refuse. That stare was not the look of a co-operative man who would listen to suggestions. Connel was about to be difficult. She was glad it was Hal who was facing that icicle of a face, not her, and after the way he'd preened himself just now she had no sympathy for Hal at all. Let Connel bite his head off. She should care.

Her sister caught her eye as she appeared back in the party. Zoe got the feeling Sancha had been watching the French windows, waiting for her while pretending to listen to the group she stood with. Zoe couldn't escape, either, because the instant she set eyes on her Sancha wiggled her way through the crowd to meet her, bursting out as they met, 'What on earth have you been up to out there with Hal Thaxford? I thought you couldn't stand the man!'

'Not you too!'

Sancha fixed her eyes on Zoe's face. 'What does that mean? Who else said something about it?'

'Oh, never mind!'

'Connel?' guessed Sancha, eyes very bright. 'I saw him go out into the garden. What did he catch you and Hal doing?'

'Nothing! Not a thing. He just has a nasty mind, that's all.' Seeing her sister smile, Zoe snapped, 'And so do you! Hal's working on my film and I wanted a chat with him about his scenes, that's all.'

'At a party!' Sancha didn't buy it, any more than Connel had. They didn't understand how much a film could obsess you—to the point where you weren't interested in anything else.

Furiously, Zoe explained. 'There's never any time to talk to actors unless you catch them in Make-up. I have so much craftwork to do…checking the set, the costumes, blocking in…'

'What?'

'Making sure the light's perfect! It takes an age because the light changes all the time—well, you know that; you're a photographer yourself. It's boring for the actors, just taking up their position, so we use extras to stand in for the stars on their mark, so we can judge the way the light hits them, how they look through the lens, if there's a shine off their make-up or something they're wearing, like earrings.'

Sancha was listening intently. They rarely discussed

filming; there was never time when they were alone. One or other of them always wanted to talk about personal problems, usually Sancha. Zoe had never had any serious personal problems. Until now.

She pulled herself up. What did she mean by that? She had no personal problems. Connel was not a problem. Nor did she intend him to be. She was staying as far away from him in future as she could.

She went on, trying to sound calm. 'Technical stuff like that is vital, but the trouble is actors always want you to tell them how to say lines, where to look, how to look. They're always asking…should I smile, should I frown? Do you want me to do this or that? Especially actors like Hal Thaxford. He constantly needs help, and then he stands there glowering in exactly the same way every time.'

'He is sexy,' Sancha said absently, but did not appear to be interested in Hal now; she seemed to have something else on her mind. Sighing she said, 'You know I'm beginning to wish I'd gone to film school instead of taking up photography. I might have been good. But it's too late now. You can't swap careers at my age.'

'Don't be so defeatist!' Zoe told her crossly. 'I hate the words "too late". It's never too late until you're dead. If you really want to be a cameraman, investigate the film schools, have an interview to see if they'll give you a place.'

Sancha shook her head wryly. 'You're forgetting—I have three children! I can't combine taking care of them with full-time training, especially as I would probably have to go to a city—London, probably—and live there while I was at college. I couldn't make that trip every day; I'd spend my life in the car or on trains.'

Zoe gave her a cynical smile. 'And, of course, Mark wouldn't hear of it!'

'I don't suppose he would, but even if he encouraged me I know I'd feel guilty about leaving the children with someone else day after day. They need me. Don't try to blame Mark, Zoe. I'm realistic about it. I can combine my local college training with looking after the kids, but if I had to travel a long way to college it would make my life quite impossible. I couldn't turn my back on them. And if I did it wouldn't make me happier, because I'd always be worrying about them. No, I'll settle for running my own business. It's exciting for both Martha and me to be taking on new responsibilities, taking a gamble. Dreams are all very well, but it's better to enjoy what you can get rather than yearn after something out of reach.'

'I suppose you're right, put like that. But I'm glad I don't have any kids! Or a husband to tell me what he thinks I should do.'

She felt a movement behind her and saw Sancha's eyes flicker, her face startled before she pulled herself together and smiled brightly.

'Oh, hallo, Connel! What a lovely party. You have a very beautiful house, too—I was saying to Zoe how much I'd love to have a room like this. It's so serene and calming.'

'Zoe didn't seem to agree,' Connel said mockingly, and she felt his warm breath drift past her bare arm. He was bending over her, his mouth almost touching her skin; she prickled with awareness. Was he going to kiss her? In front of the whole room? Her skin burned.

Sancha was staring at her; she couldn't meet her sister's eyes and looked down. What on earth must Sancha be thinking?

'I want to talk to you,' Connel said. 'Excuse us, will you, Sancha? Your sister and I have a business matter to discuss.'

What business matter? Zoe tried to think clearly but he was standing far too close. She couldn't think at all, which was increasingly disturbing. She had always prided herself on having a cool head. Now she was beginning to wonder if she had a head at all.

'Right, of course,' Sancha answered, sounding bewildered, incredulous, curious, all at once. Zoe knew how she felt. She had been feeling like that whever Connel was around for days. Weeks. It was beginning to feel like years. Time no longer had any meaning; her memory wouldn't stretch further back than the day she first met Connel.

He took her bare arm, his fingers firm and insistent, and guided her through the other guests, who watched them both with expressions rather like Sancha's. A faint buzz ran round the room; people were talking about them.

What were they saying? she wondered, flushed and self-conscious, and then, as they neared the door out into the hall, they were faced by the elegant blonde, whose long-lashed eyes swept over Zoe without warmth or friendliness.

'Problem, Connel?' she enquired, her thin, pencilled brows lifting. 'Have you got gatecrashers or something?'

He had to pause; she was blocking their way. Pretending to think her remark was a joke, which it certainly had not been—more an insult, Zoe was convinced—he laughed. 'I don't think you two know each other, do you?' he murmured. 'Bianca, this is Zoe Collins. You remember Mark? This is his sister-in-law— Sancha's sister. Zoe is a film director. You've probably seen some of her films, and she worked for TV for some time, making documentaries.'

He knew a lot about her, noted Zoe, faintly surprised because she was sure she hadn't told him much. Had he heard all this from Mark? Or from Hal Thaxford, who had given him such a critical picture of her before they ever met? What a terrifying thought—that people you had never met might have heard so much about you!

Bianca gave a graceful, chilly shrug, not even pretending an interest. 'Sorry, the name doesn't ring a bell. I'm not a big film buff and I never have time to watch television.'

Zoe wasn't surprised by any of that. People often felt they could put her down by pretending they knew nothing of films or television and cared less. As if her self-image depended on whether or not a total stranger had seen any of her work! The only people whose opinions mattered were her colleagues, her peers, who were the only people who knew what they were talking about.

There was no point in replying, though, so she laughed, instead, to make it plain she found Bianca funny; ludicrous, in fact.

Bianca didn't like that; her blue eyes iced over even more. In this undeclared war between them she had just lost a battle. So she looked Zoe over from head to toe again, stuck her nose in the air scornfully and turned away towards Connel. 'Darling, could I have a word in private before I leave? I must be off soon, and I need to tell you something. It is important.'

There was the briefest pause, then he said flatly, 'Of course. Excuse me, Zoe.' But before he walked away with Bianca he gave Zoe a hard, direct look. 'I'll talk to you later. Don't move from that spot.'

Who did he think he was? How dared he hand her orders as if she was a servant? That high-handed tone really put her back up. No way was she obeying him. It would only encourage him.

As soon as he and the blonde had left the room she hurried over to her sister and said, 'I need to get away, Sancha. I'll get a taxi. I don't want to ruin the party for you.'

Looking anxious, but not arguing, Sancha said, 'We brought you; we'll take you home. I just have to find Mark; he's talking to friends, who also work for Connel. Hang on here, I'll be back soon.'

She plunged into the crowd of guests like a ferret diving down a rabbit hole, but Zoe didn't wait. Mark's job depended on Connel; she couldn't make trouble for him. As soon as her sister had vanished Zoe hurried out of the room and asked the middle-aged woman in black, whom she found coming out of a kitchen with a platter of delicate, delicious-looking canapés, for her velvet cape.

Putting the food down, the housekeeper vanished and came back with her cape a moment later.

'Do you have the number of a good local taxi firm?' asked Zoe.

'The Star company is the best. Shall I ring for a taxi for you?'

'Thank you, would you?' She gave the housekeeper her address. 'Ask them to pick me up outside the gates, would you? A short walk in the fresh air will wake me up.'

Opening the front door, she breathed in the mild autumn scents of the garden, said goodnight, and closed the door again to begin walking down the drive, wishing she wasn't wearing those high, fragile heels. She couldn't run in them, and she was afraid Connel would find out she had left and come after her.

What can he do to you, if he does? she asked herself crossly. And, anyway, with any luck the blonde would detain him long enough to give her time to get away in her taxi. Something about the possessive way that woman had fastened on to Connel had left Zoe with the definite feeling that the other woman had designs on him, as well as his house.

Pulling her black velvet cape closer, Zoe shivered suddenly, as if a cold wind had suddenly begun to blow.

What's the matter with you? she scolded herself. Do you care whether or not the man marries the predatory blonde? What did it matter to her what he did?

With relief she heard the sound of a car approaching and turned to look down the road. There was no sign of a vehicle in either direction.

But she could still hear a car. Her heart flopped like a fish out of water as it dawned on her that the car was behind her, coming down the drive.

Maybe it was Mark and Sancha? Superstitiously, she crossed her fingers, turning to peer past the headlights to see the make of car, but she couldn't identify it, could only tell it was something sleek and red. A sports car. Not Mark's car, certainly. She had an uneasy suspicion she knew whose car it was. It drew up beside her and Connel's face loomed out of the dark interior.

'Get in!'

'Go away!' she said, desperation in her throat.

'Don't be stupid, Zoe.'

'I'm waiting for a taxi!'

'I cancelled it.'

She looked through the open window, anger blazing in her eyes. 'You did what? How dare you? You had no right!'

'Get in or I'll have to get out, pick you up and chuck you in!'

She began to walk away. The car idled beside her. Connel suddenly began to laugh, which made her angrier.

'What do you think you're doing? Going to walk all the way home, are you?'

'Shut up,' she hissed without looking at him, but he was right, of course, she was being ridiculous. In fact, she couldn't believe she was behaving this way, like some love-struck teenager incapable of dealing with how she felt. She had always had her emotions firmly under control. What had happened to her? When had she ever done anything so stupid, acted irrationally, impulsively, without caring how silly she looked?

The sports car shot ahead. He was going, leaving her. To her chagrin she felt her eyes burn with unshed tears.

Oh, stop it! she told herself. Isn't that what you want? For him to go away, leave you alone?

But she didn't know what she wanted; her mind was in total disarray, her heart completely bemused and be-wildered.

The sports car jerked to a halt a second later. Connel leapt out and loped back towards her with the lithe threat of a tiger under hot Asian skies.

She actually saw him as a tiger, his powerful muscles rippling under his white shirt, those dark eyes fixed hyp-notically on her, and couldn't move, frozen on the spot by fear and fierce attraction.

The second he reached her he picked her up, a hand under her legs, another around her waist, and lifted her off the ground.

She opened her mouth to say, Put me down! but never got the chance.

His mouth came down angrily, fiercely. Zoe's eyes shut, plunging her into darkness. Her mind went blank, but her body reacted with such intensity it terrified her. This must be how it felt to be hit by lightning. Her whole body seemed to catch fire; she was being consumed, destroyed, by agony and wild pleasure. Her hands moved without volition, ran up his chest, round his neck, fingers stroking the clenched muscles in his nape, and up into his thick, sleek hair. She kissed him back ur-gently, needing it, heard his deep groan of satisfaction.

A second later a beam of white seemed to flash behind her closed eyelids, then there was a loud, prolonged hoot which made them both jump.

Another car flashed past, still hooting. The occupants yelled something Zoe didn't, thankfully, catch.

Connel's mouth lifted, and so did his head; he began walking towards his own car a little unsteadily, as if he were drunk, but she knew it wasn't that. She knew how she felt, and if he was as off balance as she was, Connel was no longer in full control of his body, couldn't walk straight, think straight, see straight.

He bent, slid her into the passenger seat of his car, closed the door on her, walked round and got in beside her.

'Do your seat belt up,' he huskily said.

She fumbled with it and Connel lent over her to do it for her. Her intake of breath was audible; every time he came close to her she found it hard to breathe at all. Still leaning across her, he looked into her eyes; she couldn't hold his stare, her eyes drifting downwards, unable to stop herself looking at his mouth.

Connel breathed as if he was dying. She thought he was going to kiss her again and her eyes shut, her lips parted in invitation.

He groaned. 'Not yet. Not here.'

He moved away; the car burst into a deep-hearted roar and shot away. Trembling in her seat, Zoe opened her eyes. 'Don't drive so fast!' she burst out, panic-stricken.

Shooting a sideways glance at her, Connel said, 'I won't crash, don't worry. Are you still edgy after your own crash?'

She knew her voice sounded rusty; it was nothing to do with the way he was driving, or with the crash she had had. Did he know that, too? Did he know the effect he had on her?

'I suppose so.'

'You'll get over that, eventually. Have you bought a new car yet?'

'No, I'm using a hire car at the moment. I haven't

had time to look around; I'm not sure what make of car I want next.'

'Not a sports car, though?' He smiled.

'Absolutely not. I need more room than you've got in this toy car, to cart stuff around with me, things I need for work.'

'How are you getting on with your insurance claim?'

'I haven't even heard from them, so far. I sent in my claim, they sent me piles of forms to fill in—since then, silence.'

'Well, if you need a witness, give them my name.'

'I already did.'

He shot her a look, smiled. 'You aren't slow off the mark, are you?'

She watched his mouth curling in that slow, charming, teasing smile, and wanted him so intensely that it hurt to swallow.

As if he picked up what she felt, he fell silent, staring straight ahead; she stared ahead too, yet now and then sneaked a look at his hard-edged profile, temples, heavy-lidded eyes, nose, that mouth...that beautiful, sexy mouth... Oh, God, she thought, I want him more than I ever wanted anything in my life. I would give anything. Do anything. Just to have him in bed for an hour.

Her body was so hot she was a desert of burning sands. If he touched her now he would gasp with shock at the heat of her skin, she thought, silencing a half-hysterical laugh behind her hand.

Stop thinking like that! she ordered herself, but her mouth was dry as ashes. She moistened her parched lips and tasted his mouth on them where he had kissed her earlier. Closing her eyes, she let her tongue slowly caress the spot where his mouth had touched.

If only she could stop thinking about him, but her mind was alive with erotic images: his body naked, coming down, entering her...

Breathing faster and faster, her heart pounding behind her ribs, she was unaware of anything but the aroused excitement inside her, not noticing how far they had come.

When Connel's car jerked to a halt it woke her up. Her eyes widened, she looked at her cottage, then at him.

'Oh. We're...here...'

'Yes,' he said, his voice as husky as hers, then he got out of the car and came round to open the door for her. 'Got your key?'

'Yes.' She fumbled for it in her bag; Connel took it from her and strode over to open the cottage door while she was getting out of his car.

Don't ask him in! she warned herself sternly, knowing what would happen if she did. Her mind warned her not to let their relationship go too far too fast, but her mind wasn't in control of her body tonight. Her body knew what it wanted and didn't care what her mind told her.

The hall light came on, making her blink as she walked towards the open front door, spilling yellow light on to the dark drive. Connel hadn't waited to be invited in; he was already inside, holding the door open for her. She hesitated on the threshold.

She could say she was very tired, which wasn't true. She had never been so wide awake in her life.

She could say she had a headache, which wasn't true, either.

Or she could simply say that she had to be up very early next day to work and she needed a good night's sleep, which was certainly true.

But she knew, they would both know, that that was not the real, underlying reason why she didn't want him in her cottage.

'Come in,' Connel said impatiently.

Come into my parlour, said the spider to the fly. Surely no fly had ever been so desperate to be consumed? Yet common sense and self-defence wouldn't let her surrender to her own stupid instincts.

Throwing pretence to the winds, she wailed, 'No, I can't, Connel. I won't sleep with you.'

He didn't pretend to be shocked or surprised. Without answering, he picked her up, kicked the front door shut and carried her upstairs.

Zoe's mind was a battlefield. He was doing what she wanted him to do. She was dying to go to bed with him. But it was crazy. She ought to stop him. And how dared he just ignore what she had said? How dared he treat her like a doll without any right to an opinion about what happened to it, what it did?

Angrily she told him, 'If you try to make me sleep with you I'll fight you all the way!'

'I won't make you do anything, Zoe!' His voice was deep and slurred with intensity.

She shivered. 'You're not seducing me, either!'

They were in her bedroom by then. Connel lowered his face against her throat. 'Zoe...Zoe...I want you like hell.'

'You can't have me!' She hoped she sounded strong,

determined; she felt weak, yielding, utterly at his mercy. His kiss sent shudders of pleasure through her.

His mouth pushed her low neckline away, burrowed slowly, softly, down into the hollow between her breasts while he walked towards her bed and lowered her on to it, kneeled over her, kicking his shoes off, then his elegant jacket, which flew sideways on to the floor.

She desperately tried to scramble up again, and met his mouth. Demanding, coaxing, passionate, sensual, it blew her brains out.

The fight went out of her; she arched up to him, kissing him back, her hands grabbing his shirt, slipping buttons out of buttonholes, needing to touch his skin, to feel him, discover every inch of that hard, male body.

Connel groaned, 'Yes, oh, yes,' his own hands exploring, pushing her skirt upwards, stroking her bare thighs, her hips. He shrugged out of his shirt a moment later, then her dress was gone; he pulled it over her head and tossed it to the floor.

'My dress...it cost a bomb!' she groaned.

'It was the sexiest dress I've ever seen. I couldn't take my eyes off you all evening,' he muttered, his head moving down her body, kissing her breasts while he unclipped her bra and removed it. Kissing her naked midriff, pulling down her lacy panties, he whispered, 'But what was under it is much sexier.'

She caught hold of his head, her hands filled with his black hair, the rough strands tickling her palm. 'You're going too fast!' Her voice was shaky with a muddle of need, uncertainty, panic.

'If I don't have you soon I'll go out of my mind,' he

said, kicking his trousers and then his briefs off. Now they were both naked, staring at each other.

It only lasted a second or two, that instant of confrontation, finally seeing each other without disguises or clothes; Zoe looked at his broad shoulders and deep chest, that slim waist, strong hips and what lay between them.

She shut her eyes after one glance, then, burning with desire, fell back against the pillows.

Breathing roughly, his heart audibly beating too fast, Connel came down on top of her, pushing her legs apart, moving between them, his hands caressing her smooth thighs as he lifted her slightly to open her for his entry.

She was shivering, tense; she felt like a virgin. He was the first, in a very real sense. The first man she had ever loved. The first man she had ever wanted so much she was dying for him, had to have him inside her. Suddenly she knew what sex really was—not just some passing pleasure, but a necessity, an emptiness he had to fill, only him, no other man.

She took him into herself with a long moan of satisfaction, completing herself at last. It was a miracle the way he fitted so exactly into her. They had been made for each other. After years apart now they finally came together again.

They made love with an urgency that was intolerable; bodies writhing, entwined, moving in hot tension, her arms and legs around him, his body a driving force inside her, thrusting deeper and deeper. Zoe cried out feverishly at the end, not even knowing what she was saying, or doing.

Afterwards, Connel collapsed on top of her, his face against her neck, his chest rising and falling breathlessly.

Her bedroom was dark except for a faint glimmer of moonlight which slid across the carpet.

Her skin was damp with perspiration, her pulses hammered, her heart was beating like the drum of a retreating army, irregularly, too fast.

Connel slowly slid off her, stood up, pulled the duvet cover at the foot of the bed over her and got back on to the bed. Turning her slightly so that her back was towards him, he slid his arm around her waist, moving tightly in against her, a hand below her breasts, one thigh crossing hers, locking them together.

His voice whispered into her nape, his breath stirring the tendrils of red hair. 'Did you mean that?'

'What?' she drowsily asked, limp and warm in his embrace.

'Never mind, you can say it again in the morning.'

Zoe fell asleep, body and mind utterly exhausted.

CHAPTER TEN

ZOE woke up with a start and for a few seconds was disorientated. Her alarm wasn't ringing; the room was in pitch-darkness. What had woken her up? Yawning, she leaned over to pick up her clock, peered at the glowing phosphorescent hands and saw it was eleven o'clock.

Putting the clock down, she lay back, intending to sleep again, only to hear a car engine start outside on her drive. What on earth was that?

Her mind jangled with surprise and shock. She had forgotten last night until that instant, but now it all rushed back—the party, driving here in Connel's car, and what had happened, in this room, in her bed.

He had been in it with her when she went to sleep. She didn't need to look to know he wasn't there now.

She slid out of bed and ran to the window. The taillights of his car were just disappearing through her gates.

Leaning on the windowsill, Zoe stared after them, her mind dissolving in pain and bewilderment.

Why was he going? Where was he going?

After making love to her so passionately he had let her fall asleep, in his arms, then he had silently detached himself, stolen from her bed, got dressed in the dark, gone downstairs, let himself out of the front door and driven away.

A cynical little voice inside her said—Well, he'd had

what he wanted, hadn't he? Why should he stay around after that?

From that first night when they met he had probably had his sights set on getting her. Remember what he had said? Remember the impression of her Hal Thaxford had given him? Connel had picked up the idea that she was some sort of challenge to his sex. Had he decided to take up that challenge, beat her at what he saw as her own game?

All these weeks, had he been stalking her with the intention of getting her into bed?

She closed her eyes, groaning, covered her face with her trembling hands.

Hal had told him she dated men, then dumped them ruthlessly. Was that what Connel had planned for her?

That wouldn't be enough for him, though, would it? Having beaten her at her own game, he would need to tell people. Tell Hal, anyway! The idea of the two men talking about her, laughing, gloating, made her sick.

She couldn't bear it. Her mind cringed in misery and pain.

There was no chance of sleep again. Putting on a warm, woollen dressing gown, because she was as cold as ice now, she went downstairs.

Maybe he had left a note? A little spark of hope lit inside her, but there was nothing.

She made herself a pot of coffee, sat up with it, crouching in front of the electric fire, staring into the glowing red bars, remembering and wincing at the pain of her memories, brooding on what Connel might do next, while she drank cup after cup of the strong, black coffee.

She must not let him destroy her. Somehow she had to restore her pride, hide what she felt.

Before the sun came up she had showered, dressed in her working clothes, and was on her way to the location site. She was tense at having gone without sleep, so wound up over how she felt about Connel she was like a puppet on wires, jangling mentally and physically. How was she going to get through the day?

Will and the others were soon aware of her mood. They gave her wary looks as they jumped to obey her. The actors lurked in their caravans as much as possible; the production staff ran like rabbits, bolt-eyed in alarm in case she turned her icy rage on them. Luckily, there was a great deal to do that morning; she didn't have time to think about her personal life, because her work kept her fully occupied.

As the day wore on she was so engrossed in the scene they were shooting that her mind never wandered from the usual problems of making sure the technical machinery was working perfectly. In filming, there was always something going wrong. The sound man kept complaining about traffic noise in the distance, about a plane flying overhead, about a flock of wood pigeons that flew into the trees and began cooing to each other. Will was groaning because although the sun was bright at times there were clouds passing overhead which kept the light changing every minute or so. A filter he used didn't help much, either. Then one of the cables suddenly started giving off sparks and burst into flames. Will rushed to grab a fire extinguisher, sprayed the burning cable with bubbling, white foam. The fire was put out, but that area of the location was then full of floating foam, and had to be cleared up before they could start filming.

Before that, however, they broke for lunch—the catering van had thin slices of ham with salad, or spaghetti with tomato, red pepper and broccoli sauce for vegetarians. There were sandwiches, too, wrapped in plastic film. Zoe had a salad sandwich and an apple. She ate with Will, who had a huge plate of spaghetti, eying her sandwich with disapproval.

'That won't give you much energy! You're too thin. A woman should have a few curves.'

'Mind your own business and eat your own lunch. Now, listen, in the call sheet I noticed that…' She broke off, green eyes narrowing as she spotted Hal Thaxford peering at her from behind a group of other actors clustering around the food wagon. 'So he is here!' she muttered to herself.

Giving her a surprised look, Will picked up his pink schedule, flicked an eye down the cast list pinned to it. 'Hal? Isn't he supposed to be working with us this week? He's on my list—we should get to his scene this afternoon, if we're lucky. At the rate we've been going so far! I thought we might have finished shooting Scene 43 by now.'

'It's been one of those days,' she absently murmured, becoming aware that Hal was sidling towards them. Had Connel said anything to him when he arrived back at the party? Or had Hal gone by the time Connel got there? It must have been late. Half past eleven? She felt hot colour creeping up her face and bent her head over her script. She would know the minute she met Hal's eyes, but she was in no hurry to find out. If Hal did know what had happened last night he would have started spreading the gossip by now, and she would hear the echo of it sooner or later.

Will gave her a sideways look, eyes concerned. 'Certainly has. What's wrong, Zoe? You've been snapping like a crocodile since you arrived.'

She didn't deny it. 'Sorry. Just an off day, I guess.'

'Private life or is it one of those female things?' grunted Will without looking at her again, concentrating on his spaghetti, which was disappearing at an amazing rate. For someone who was so thin and wiry, Will ate large amounts. He used up so many calories in his work; cameras were pretty heavy, although as Will often gratefully said they were much lighter today than they had been when he trained. Some of them were feather-light, in fact, but Will had developed enormous muscles from carrying cameras and equipment about when he was younger.

She admired Will. He was good. Very good. He had worked with some amazing people: directors she respected, actors she would love to work with herself.

'I have a personal problem,' she muttered.

He looked up, watched her. 'Anything you can talk about?'

She shook her head. 'No, too private.'

'It helps to talk these things out. Helps you think more clearly. I care a lot about you, Zoe, you know that.'

She knew, and was sad. Will had been chasing her for a long time but she would never see him as anything but a buddy.

'Thanks, Will,' she said softly. 'You're one of my best friends, too.'

He grimaced. 'Just a friend, though?'

She put a hand on top of one of his. 'What do you mean, just a friend? How many really good friends have you got? I know I haven't got many.'

Will looked at her hand, took it into both his, looking at her soberly. 'You've changed lately. You're different. Gentler, sweeter…are you in love, Zoe? Is that it?'

She flushed, then went white, pulling her hand free, but before she needed to answer someone else joined them.

'Hi.'

Hal's voice made her stiffen. She summoned up a cool smile, lifting her head to meet his eyes.

She knew the second she looked into them that Connel hadn't yet told him. Hal couldn't act well enough to hide such knowledge. That handsome wooden face hid nothing.

'Hi, Hal.' Her voice was rough with relief. She felt Will's attention. He had picked up on her tone, but he thought she was simply irritated by Hal, as usual. Out of the corner of her eye she caught his suppressed, amused smile.

Hal was looking reproachful. 'I came over to tell you I managed to talk to Connel…' His expression glowed with self-satisfaction. 'And he will let us use the rose garden, so long as there's a written contract guaranteeing him against damage or expense.'

She had forgotten all about that idea, and after last night was no longer sure she wanted to go ahead with it.

'I'll talk to the company about a contract,' she slowly

said, then smiled at Hal, deliberately using charm. 'Thanks, Hal. I'm very grateful.'

'That's okay, my pleasure,' he said, then hesitated. 'When do you think you'll get round to my scene?'

She waved a hand at Will. 'Ask the master.'

'Later this afternoon,' guessed Will.

Hal sighed, nodded. 'Well, I'll get into the card game, then.' A group of actors and crew not needed on set at the moment were playing cards in one of the caravans.

Since it wasn't politic for Zoe to know about the card game, she didn't comment. If anyone from the film company found out she permitted it she would get a load of trouble. They would object to paying people to sit around playing cards, although they were aware of the long hours spent setting up every scene and must realise that the actors were often kept hanging around waiting most of the day. Actors read, knitted, embroidered, exercised, gossiped, played cards or dominoes or chess, did anything to pass the time. As long as they didn't get in her way she didn't care what they did.

When Hal had gone Will shot her a curious look. 'What was all that about?'

She didn't quite meet his eyes. Casually, she said, 'Oh, I had an idea yesterday—Hal and I were at a party in his cousin's house...'

Will's brows shot up. 'You and Hal went to a party together? I had no idea you were dating him. My God, don't tell me you're in love with Hal Thaxford! You can't be that stupid!'

'That isn't funny!' She grimaced, flushing. 'You know what I think of Hal. We were both at the same party, that's all.'

'Yeah?' drawled Will, and she laughed crossly.

'Yes! I went with my sister and her husband, who works for Hal's cousin.' Why was she explaining? What had her private life to do with Will?

'Who's that? The cousin?' Will had finished his spaghetti and was eating a pear which he had peeled carefully first.

She took an unsteady breath, afraid that just saying his name might give her away.

'His name's Hillier. Connel Hillier.' She had got the name out without stumbling or stammering; relief made her run on easily. 'He runs a civil engineering firm and he has this beautiful house, near a village called Rookby…'

'Are there any?'

'What?' Interrupted again, she was thrown, staring at Will blankly.

'Rooks?'

'I've no idea. It was dark when we got there, dark when we left. Anyway, Hal and I talked about his part in the film, out in the garden…'

'In the dark?' Will was amused, curious, teasing again.

She glared. 'Don't try to make anything of it. There's nothing to make. There were other people exploring the garden, and it was very overcrowded in the house, so we went out for some fresh air and found this sunken rose garden.'

'You're very touchy on the subject of Hal! You're making me jealous. Are you hiding something?'

'Of course I'm not.' Not about Hal, anyway. Luckily, it hadn't occurred to him that Hal's cousin might be

behind her edginess. 'And I'm not touchy about Hal.
Will you listen? This sunken garden had high red brick
walls, trellises of roses, lots of them still in bloom—it
was quite lovely, and it occurred to me that it would
make a great setting for the love scene between Hal and
Lindsay.'

Will flipped the pages of his shooting script, found
the right scene, read it, frowning. 'Well, it would certainly be a good idea to vary the background; it adds
depth. I always like a new background, myself, and it
would fit the storyline. But can we afford it? How much
will this guy charge? That's the question.'

'Hal didn't mention money.'

'If his cousin's a businessman, his lawyers will, when
the contract is drawn up. What's it worth to get a different background?'

'We'll see what he wants first, then decide. We won't
get to that scene for about ten days.' She looked at her
watch. 'Look at the time! Let's get on, Will.'

When she got home that evening she was on tenter-
hooks, half expecting to see Connel's car parked outside,
but there was no sign of him. The first thing she did, as
usual, when she got inside, was to turn on the answer-
machine for her messages.

The calls were mostly work-related, but the third
voice was Sancha's.

'Okay, so what happened? Why did you run out like
that? Mark was angry. We brought you and it was his
boss's house—it was insulting to Connel, and the last
thing he wants is for you to upset Connel. Ring me. I
want to hear all about it, Zoe!'

Not on your life, thought Zoe, as her sister's voice ended. She wasn't telling Sancha anything.

The machine whirred and she found herself listening to Philip Cross, the company accountant, making his almost daily call of complaint about her spending.

'You're over budget again, Zoe. We don't have unlimited cash; this isn't Hollywood. That party scene, the fancy dress…who ran those costumes up? What do you have wardrobe women for if it isn't to make low-budget costumes? You didn't have to hire them from London. And there are too many vehicles being used. You can cut down the number of cars, surely…'

Half-listening, half-wishing he was here and she could tell him what she thought of him, she sat down to eat her hurriedly assembled meal—a slice of grilled fresh salmon, some salad, some fruit.

She had finished her fish by the time Philip had stopped moaning on about costs. Zoe reached for her glass of orange juice, only to have her hand start shaking and knock it over as Connel's voice came on the machine.

Leaping up, she stood the glass upright again, grabbed a dishcloth and began moping the table, her pulses beating behind her ears, at her neck and wrists. She loved that deep, cool, male voice. The sound of it made her tremble.

'Zoe, I have to go abroad,' he said curtly and impersonally, as if she was one of his office staff. 'No idea when I'll get back.' The answer-machine buzzed and whirred, breaking up into sea noises, out of which his distant voice said, 'See you.' Then the machine clicked off and Zoe sat down before her knees gave way under her.

That wasn't how lovers spoke to each other. There had been nothing personal, nothing passionate, in that tone.

He didn't care two pins about her.

That was obvious. She had suspected it when she'd found he had gone without leaving a note. Now she was sure about it. They had slept together, now he was walking out without looking back.

Anger, shame, humiliation washed over her in hot waves. She couldn't sit there. Jumping up, she began clearing the table, tidying the kitchen. Then went up to bed and worked for an hour on tomorrow's scenes before she put out the light.

Amazingly, she slept. Probably because she hadn't slept much last night and was so stressed and exhausted that she couldn't stay awake. She dreamt, though. All night she woke briefly from dreams of running after Connel as he vanished, hurrying through rooms she did not recognise, searching for him, seeing him at a distance, but always going away from her and not looking back. She always went back to sleep without difficulty, back to those dreams, that misery.

She woke in tears, on a damp pillow, and sensed she had cried more than once during the night.

Was this how it felt to have your heart broken? She had never believed in breaking hearts. She had laughed the idea to scorn. Hearts do not break. They are organs of the body; they function like machines; pump, pump, beat, beat, lubbadub, lubbadub, they go, sending the blood through your veins, keeping you alive. They do not break.

But hers had. She was one of the walking dead, a zombie moving automatically without knowing what she was doing. Without a heart, without a brain.

For the rest of that week she buried herself in work. She heard nothing from Connel, but the company lawyers let her know they had made a deal with Connel's lawyer over the use of the rose garden. He had asked only for a returnable deposit to cover possible damage or nuisance. If the film crew behaved impeccably the deposit would be paid back. The lawyers were pleased with their negotiations, and so was Philip Cross, the accountant.

'Just make sure no damage is done and the man can't sue us!' his voice nagged on her answer-machine.

Hal told her Connel was in the Argentine on business. 'And probably chatting up dark-eyed *señoritas*, if I know him!' he grinned.

Zoe grinned back, the skin around her mouth stiff, jealousy burning inside her chest, although Hal couldn't know that, unless Connel had now told him about the night of the party, but she didn't think he had; she didn't read anything in Hal's manner or his eyes.

Later she snapped at him, 'For God's sake, Hal, could you try to talk as if you were a man, not a recorded phone message!'

He glared. Hal was good at glaring. He did it even when he wasn't trying. It was probably his natural expression. She wouldn't be surprised to hear that his face fell into glaring, brooding lines even when he was asleep. His fans loved it, loved the smouldering stares, the locked jawline, the rough masculine voice.

'I'm only saying my lines!'

She sweetened her voice, sarcastically said, 'I don't want you to only say them. I want you to act, Hal. I know it's hard—but could you try? I know you went to drama school. They must have taught you something.'

There were indrawn breaths all round them. Eyes widened, people looked at each other, open-mouthed.

How could she say such a thing to Hal? Of all people! One of the best-loved actors on TV? Hal's mouth had dropped open; he couldn't believe it, either.

'We'll go again,' she said. 'Marks, everybody. Okay, Will? Okay, sound? Everybody ready? Hal, stop sulking.'

'Stop nagging,' he muttered, so low she barely heard him.

'What did you say?'

'Nothing,' he said, acting—brilliantly, for once—the part of an innocent man wrongly accused. 'Just rehearsing my lines.'

She knew she was behaving like a bear with a sore head. She couldn't help it. Being in love, she discovered, is like toothache—once you've got it you can't forget it. It nags on and on in the back of your mind, whatever you're doing, hurting intolerably.

It had never happened to Zoe before, and she didn't know how to cope. How did you disguise constant pain? How did you keep smiling when you wanted to cry? How did you stop yelling at people, complaining, losing your temper over nothing? Why had she never realised love could destroy you like this?

That Saturday she had lunch with Sancha and Mark. Sancha had tried out recipes from a book of Spanish cooking Mark had bought her, beginning with a large dish of tapas, tiny saucers each containing a different food. Artichokes dressed with vinaigrette, tiny fried whitebait fish, boiled eggs stuffed with anchovies or tuna in tomato sauce, prawns. The main course was a casserole Sancha called Chicken Andaluz. Breast of chicken had been cooked for a couple of hours slowly, with bacon pieces, tomato, red peppers and slices of hot spicy red sausage.

'*Chorizo al diablo,*' Mark told her. 'Devilled sausage to you.' He was learning Spanish because they had rented a villa in Marbella for a fortnight next spring, and Mark was determined to be able to talk to shopkeepers and waiters in restaurants.

'Devilled sausage to you, too,' Zoe said, tasting a piece. 'Mmm, delicious,' she told her sister. 'I must try cooking *chorizo* some time. You can use it on pizzas, can't you?'

'Pity you can't cook,' teased Mark.

Coldly she informed him, 'I can cook. I just never have the time.'

'And nobody to cook for,' murmured Mark.

Sancha looked uneasy. 'I'll get the pudding,' she said, getting up to begin clearing the table.

Zoe went with her, partly to get away from Mark's teasing, and partly so that she could talk alone with her sister.

As they loaded the dishwasher in the kitchen Sancha said, 'Did you know Connel was in South America again?'

Zoe kept her face averted, feeding cutlery into the tray at the top of the machine. 'Yes, I had heard.'

'Mark thinks he's planning another of his expeditions—Connel loves South America. I suppose running a business here isn't as exciting as traveling around hot, exotic places. But it makes things difficult for Mark because when Connel's out of touch it can hold up decisions. Mark can handle most things, but where big money is concerned he needs Connel's agreement before he can sign a deal.'

Zoe felt like breaking down in tears. So Connel was planning another long trip abroad? She couldn't bear the thought of never seeing him again, but she had to hide it from her sister and brother-in-law. Had to smile and smile however much it hurt. The thought of Sancha and Mark realising how she felt was unbearable.

After all she had said about men and the folly of falling in love—how could she admit that she had fallen hard, at last, for a man who didn't feel the same?

'Mark suspects he's running away,' Sancha said.

Zoe stiffened. 'What does that mean? Running away from what?'

'From whom, you mean! Mark says Bianca has her sights set on him. Keeps ringing up, turning up at the office on transparent pretexts. If Connel isn't careful he'll end up marrying her, so he's decided to leave the country!'

'Wouldn't it be easier just to make it clear he doesn't want to marry her?' Zoe said angrily. Why did Bianca think Connel might marry her? Had he slept with her too?

'You met her. Do you think she'd meekly disappear?'

'If he was blunt enough, what else could she do?'

Sancha gave her an incredulous glance. 'What you
know about human nature could be written on the back
of a postage stamp, couldn't it? Women like that don't
take no for an answer. Connel's rich and sexy. Of course
she isn't going to give up hope just because he says he
doesn't want to get married. In fact, she would take his
saying that as a come-on. Mention marriage and you're
admitting the possibility. She's the bloodhound type.
Connel's probably wise to flee the country.'

Zoe brooded over that as she drove home that evening
towards her cold, lonely cottage. Would Connel even
come back? She might never see him again. She stared
out through the windscreen at passing headlights, barely
noticing anything.

Autumn gales had hit their part of the country that
afternoon, rattling windows, howling through bare trees,
filling the gutters with the last brown leaves, twigs,
fallen branches, making driving difficult and even dangerous. She shivered as she dashed from her car into the
house, then froze as she heard a sound behind her. There
was someone lurking in the darkness.

Not Larry again! she thought, and put on a burst of
speed in the hope of getting into the house before he
caught up with her.

'It's me, Zoe!' a voice said from the dark as she got
to the front door, and she stopped dead, recognising it,
turned sharply, a hot pulse going in her throat.

She couldn't believe it for a second, staring fixedly as
his tall figure came closer, his eyes glinting in the darkness of his face.

She swallowed. 'You're back.' Her voice sounded so

flat and calm, she was astonished by it. Nobody would ever guess what was happening inside her, the wild turmoil of her blood, the weakness of her legs, the desire leaping like fire through her flesh.

'Where have you been? I've been waiting here for a couple of hours. Saturday is your day off. I thought you would be at home.'

'I had lunch with Sancha and Mark.'

They were talking casually, as if they were acquaintances. Was that how he thought of her? As someone he barely knew?

Barely, she thought, trembling. He knew her naked and dressed. Inside and out.

'Damn it. I thought of ringing Mark but I didn't want to talk about work and I didn't know if you had told them about us.'

'Us?' she repeated, shivering as the gale blew and trees bent and swayed like drunks.

Connel's eyes focused intently on her pale face. 'It's cold out here. Shall we go in or aren't you going to invite me in tonight?'

She looked at him helplessly, tears burning in her eyes. 'Go away, Connel. Just go away. I'm too tired to cope with you tonight.'

'Why are you crying?'

'I'm not!'

'I can see the tears in your eyes, hear them in your voice!'

'Go away, go away,' she yelled, swung and tried to open her front door, but couldn't get the key into the lock because her hands were shaking too much.

Shouldering her aside, Connel took the key and

opened the door. She tried to rush inside, before he could, but he was immediately behind her and still had her key. He closed the front door, shutting out the howling wind, put on the light and she flinched from it, covering her eyes with one hand.

'Look, I'm tired. I want you to go!' There was a lot more she wanted to say but dared not start to say in case she broke down like a child and sobbed and wailed in front of him. Her pride wouldn't let her do that. He mustn't know just how much she cared.

He walked past her and she heard him switch on the central heating, then there was the sound of water running as he filled a kettle. He knew where everything was in her house; he knew the place almost as well as she did.

She shed her sheepskin coat, hung it up, walked slowly, reluctantly, into the kitchen.

'I thought you were in the Argentine.'

'I was. Now I'm here.' He intended to make tea, had the teapot set out on a tray with cups, milk and a sugar bowl; he always did everything so swiftly and efficiently.

'Sancha thought you might be planning to stay there.'

'Oh, did she? Your sister has a busy imagination, doesn't she? She's way off with my future plans, though. My trip to the Argentine was strictly business. I was over there to check out a contract which is up for tender—a major civil engineering project worth millions. I've decided to go for it.'

'So Sancha wasn't wrong at all! If you're planning to get involved in work over there you'll have to live there.'

'Not necessarily. I shall delegate. Mark speaks Spanish.'

'Mark?' She was taken aback, stared at him open-mouthed for a minute, thinking through the implications, then burst out, 'But what about Sancha and the children? He'd either have to leave them behind or uproot them all, and Sancha is just about to start a whole new career, and the children don't speak Spanish and...'

Impatiently, Connel interrupted, 'We may not even get the contract, and if we do I'll talk things over with Mark before I make any decisions.'

'Mind my own business, you mean!' she muttered. 'But Sancha and the kids are my business. I love them and I don't want to see their lives blown apart.'

'Don't you think Mark will make sure that doesn't happen? That marriage strikes me as pretty sound. I'm sure he'll discuss it with Sancha before he comes to a decision about going to the Argentine.'

She snapped at him, 'Mark is an old-fashioned male—he thinks it's up to him to make decisions about his job. I don't think he will take Sancha's career plans very seriously.'

The water had boiled. He made the tea, covered the pot with a padded cosy, took the tray over to the table while she watched, thinking that the man was astonishingly domesticated for someone so tough and male. 'It still isn't your problem, Zoe,' he told her over his shoulder. 'It's Mark and Sancha's decision. Haven't you got enough worries of your own without taking on your sister's?'

'Snap,' she said belligerently. 'You keep telling me what to do—why don't you take your own advice and mind your own business? Just go away and leave me alone, will you?'

He swung and caught hold of her arms, pulled her towards him before she had notice of his intention.

'No,' he said roughly, and she looked up into eyes like black holes in space and was silenced by the intensity of his stare.

'You aren't dumping me, Zoe, I won't let you,' he said, his voice thick and angry, then his head came down and his mouth moved hungrily against hers, the force of his kiss pushing her head back, so that she had to grab at him to stay upright.

He let go of her arms and framed her face between his hands, his kiss deepening, pushing her lips apart. Zoe's arms went round his neck. She stood on tiptoe to kiss him back, past trying to hide anything, giving in to her desire for him.

He was muttering something against her mouth. For a second she couldn't make out what he was saying, then she caught the words.

'I love you, damn you. I love you.'

She began to cry and his head lifted. He stared down at her with that scary intensity.

Hoarsely, he groaned, 'I shouldn't have said it. I knew it would be a mistake to tell you how I felt. I couldn't help myself. Zoe, I warn you—if you try and dump me I won't be responsible for what I do.'

Tears running down her face, she leaned on him weakly, her hands on his nape, fingers digging into his thick black hair.

'I love you, stupid,' she told him. 'Can't you tell? I'm crazy about you.'

Connel made a deep, passionate sound in his throat, then his head swooped again and their mouths met. Their bodies clung so tightly that you couldn't have got a piece of paper between them.

When he finally stopped kissing her Connel gazed down at her again intently.

'Will you marry me, Zoe?'

She didn't even hesitate. 'Yes, please,' she said, and briefly imagined Sancha's face when she told her.

HARLEQUIN PRESENTS®

THE BARONS

One sister, three brothers— who will inherit, and will they all find lovers?

Jonas is approaching his eighty-fifth birthday, and he's decided it's time to choose the heir of his sprawling ranch, Espada. He has three ruggedly good-looking sons, Gage, Travis and Slade, and a beautiful stepdaughter, Caitlin.

Who will receive Baron's bequest? As the Baron brothers and their sister discover, there's more at stake than Espada. For love also has its part to play in deciding their futures....

Enjoy Gage's story:
Marriage on the Edge
Harlequin Presents #2027, May 1999

And in August, get to know Travis a whole lot better in
More than a Mistress
Harlequin Presents #2045

Available wherever Harlequin books are sold.

HARLEQUIN®
Makes any time special ™

Look us up on-line at: http://www.romance.net   HPBARON

Looking For More Romance?

Visit Romance.net

Look us up on-line at: http://www.romance.net

**Check in daily for these and
other exciting features:**

Hot off
the press

View all
current titles,
and purchase
them on-line.

**What do the
stars have in
store for you?**

Horoscope

Hot
deals

Exclusive offers
available only at
Romance.net

Plus, don't miss our interactive quizzes,
contests and bonus gifts.

PWEB

HARLEQUIN ◆ PRESENTS®

Jarrett, Jonathan and Jordan are

BACHELOR BROTHERS

An exhilarating new miniseries by favorite author

CAROLE MORTIMER

The Hunter brothers are handsome, wealthy and
determinedly single—until each meets the woman
of his dreams. But dates and diamonds aren't
enough to win her heart.
Are those bachelor boys about to become husbands?

Find out in:
To Woo a Wife
Harlequin Presents® #2039, July 1999

To Be a Husband
#2043, August 1999

To Be a Bridegroom
#2051, September 1999

Some men are *meant* to marry!

Available wherever Harlequin books are sold.

HARLEQUIN®
Makes any time special ™

Look us up on-line at: http://www.romance.net   HPBBROS

HARLEQUIN PRESENTS®

*invites you to see
how the other half marry in*

SOCIETY WEDDINGS

This sensational new five-book miniseries invites you to be our VIP guest at some of the most talked-about weddings of the decade—spectacular events where the cream of society gather to celebrate the marriages of dazzling brides and grooms in breathtaking, international locations.

Be there to toast each of the happy couples:

Aug. 1999—**The Wedding-Night Affair,** #2044, Miranda Lee

Sept. 1999—**The Impatient Groom,** #2054, Sara Wood

Oct. 1999—**The Mistress Bride,** #2056, Michelle Reid

Nov. 1999—**The Society Groom,** #2066, Mary Lyons

Dec. 1999—**A Convenient Bridegroom,** #2067, Helen Bianchin

Available wherever Harlequin books are sold.

HARLEQUIN®

Makes any time special ™

Look us up on-line at: http://www.romance.net

HPSOCW

Celebrate **15** years with

HARLEQUIN®

I N T R I G U E®

Because romance is the ultimate mystery...

*It's been 15 years since Harlequin Intrigue®
premiered—and we're still leaving you
breathless with pulse-pounding suspense
that heightens and electrifies romance to
keep you on the edge of your seat.*

Check your retail outlet for some of your favorite
Intrigue® authors and books!

✔ **43 LIGHT STREET** by Rebecca York
✔ **FEAR FAMILIAR** by Caroline Burnes
✔ **THE LANDRY BROTHERS**—a *new* series
   from Kelsey Roberts
✔ **COUNTDOWN 2000**—a special millennium
   promotion from three of your favorite authors!

Dynamic life-and-death stories with a
happy ending that you can find only at

HARLEQUIN®

I N T R I G U E®

HARLEQUIN®
Makes any time special ™

Look us up on-line at: http://www.romance.net   HI15ANNIV

Coming Next Month

HARLEQUIN PRESENTS®

THE BEST HAS JUST GOTTEN BETTER!

**#2049 MISTRESS BY ARRANGEMENT Helen Bianchin
(Presents Passion)**
Michelle is stunned when wealthy businessman
Nikos Alessandros asks her to be his social companion for a
few weeks. Will Michelle, under pressure from her family to
make a suitable marriage, find herself becoming a mistress
by arrangement?

**#2050 HAVING LEO'S CHILD Emma Darcy
(Expecting!)**
Leo insisted she marry him for the sake of their unborn child.
But despite his fiery kisses, Teri couldn't forget that Leo had
never considered marrying her before she got pregnant.
Could they turn great sex into eternal love?

**#2051 TO BE A BRIDEGROOM Carole Mortimer
(Bachelor Brothers)**
Jordan is the youngest Hunter brother. His devilish good
looks have helped him seduce any woman he's ever wanted—
except Stazy. There's only one way for Jordan to get to the
head of Stazy's queue—become a bridegroom!

#2052 A HUSBAND OF CONVENIENCE Jacqueline Baird
When an accident left Josie with amnesia, she assumed that
her gorgeous husband, Conan, was the father of her unborn
baby. They shared passionate nights until she remembered
that theirs was actually a marriage of convenience....

#2053 WEDDING-NIGHT BABY Kim Lawrence
Georgina decided she couldn't attend her ex-fiancé's wedding alone—she needed an escort! Callum Stewart was
perfect: gorgeous, dynamic...and on the night of the
wedding he became the father of her child!

**#2054 THE IMPATIENT GROOM Sara Wood
(Society Weddings)**
Prince Rozzano di Barsini whisked Sophia Charlton away to
Venice in his private jet. One whirlwind seduction later, she'd
agreed to be his bride. But why was Rozzano in such a hurry
to marry? Because he needed an heir...?

HARLEQUIN · FIVE DECADES OF ROMANCE · CELEBRATES

Starting in September 1999, Harlequin Temptation® will also be celebrating an anniversary—15 years of bringing you the best in passion.

Look for these Harlequin Temptation® titles at your favorite retail stores in September:

CLASS ACT
by Pamela Burford

BABY.COM
by Molly Liholm

NIGHT WHISPERS
by Leslie Kelly

THE SEDUCTION OF SYDNEY
by Jamie Denton

Look us up on-line at: http://www.romance.net   H50HT/L